THE LAST DAYS

AND

THE GREAT TRIBULATION

BY

JEFF BRADLEY STERN

The Last Days and The Great Tribulation

A short story by

Jeff Bradley Stern

The Last Days and The Great Tribulation

Jeff Bradley Stern

Published by CreateSpace
www.CreateSpace.com
Copyright 2010 Jeff Stern
All rights reserved.

ISBN – 978-0615644523

Contact author for reproduction requests, comments, or corrections at
Clintons@comcast.net

THE LAST DAYS AND THE GREAT TRIBULATION

"for then there will be great tribulation such as has not occurred since the world's beginning until now, no, nor will occur again." -Matthew 24:21

„The Last Days and The Great Tribulation" is a fictional short story set in America in the year 2014 that follows our two leading characters from their high school years onward, as they live through The prophetic occurrence, foretold long ago in the bible.

IMPORTANT NOTE:

"Concerning that day and hour nobody knows, neither the angels of the heavens nor the Son, but only the Father."
-Matthew 24:36
The author is not predicting a definite period in time for the great tribulation to occur. He chose the future because the great tribulation has YET to occur!

"This know also, that in the last days perilous times shall come. For men shall be lovers of their own selves, covetous, boasters, proud, blasphemers, disobedient to parents, unthankful, unholy, without natural affection, trucebreakers, false accusers, incontinent, fierce, despisers of those that are good, traitors, heady, highminded, lovers of pleasures more than lovers of God; having a form of godliness, but denying the power thereof: from such turn away. Ever learning, and never able to come to the knowledge of the truth."
2 Timothy 3: 1-5, 7
King James Version

Table Of Contents

CHAPTER ONE

THE LAST DAYS

In his dressing room at the Ahmanson theatre in Los Angeles, California; Daniel Lucas Devoreaux Jones waits pensively for the call to go onstage. There's been a delay in the shows scheduled start due to technical difficulties. There's a buzz backstage and throughout the entire theatre; an electricity in the air that is effervescently hypnotic. Yet on an evening that would for most entertainers be the happiest night of their career he couldn't have been more ill at ease. Devoreaux D. Jones, his stage name, known to his fans as D Jones, is to be honored tonight as the only pop star in entertainment history to have a top forty, number one hit song, based on an opera aria.

At the tender age of sixteen he soared with meteoric momentum to the acme of the music and entertainment industry. In a modernized makeover of a standard vehicle, he whimsically imparted the invigorating breath of life into an old classic, which made him an overnight sensation. Even now at the age of thirty-three, with an extensive track record of top ten hit songs of various styles, and while yet no longer possessing the voice of a boy soprano, the opera world has not forgotten his debut achievement of bringing opera to the masses. Tonight they are rekindling their love affair with D.

His thoughts however are light years away from tonight's affair; but with close friends who are under obdurate scrutiny by government officials.
„How had the world gotten this far, so fast, in making criminals out of those who participate in activity, that only a year ago was considered the cornerstone for the right to freedom in America?", he rhetorically asks himself.
He sits there alone, staring straight ahead deep in his thoughts when a knock on the door jolts him back to the reality of the theatre.
„Fifty minutes Mr. Jones", rang out the man's voice, almost as if sung, from the other side of his dressing room door.

D extracts himself from the black leather sofa that seemingly engulfs his slender athletic frame. Before walking over to the dressing table he pours himself a cup of blackberry tea from his Thermos. As he sits bathed in the radiant luminescence of the lights circumvallating the mirrors on the white dressing table, he double checks his appearance and takes a sip from the cup of piping hot tea. He then picks up the telephone and orders a gin Martini from the bar to calm his unsettled and slightly unsteady nerves before the show.

As with so many of these supercilious socialite events while alone before the show he reflects on a time when his life was less complex. Like the quiet before the storm are these tranquil moments before ShowTime when he sneaks musingly out the backstage door of his mind's eye to his childhood in junior high school. D smiles at his reflection in the mirror as he thinks to himself, „Yeah......., that's where and when it really all began. "

* * * *

Outside of the massive Oakwood doors of the high school auditorium Daniel tarries in eager anticipation wondering what kind of response his presence will generate when discovered standing about a stone's throw away from the entrance where the high school talent contest was about to finish. His large dovelike hazel colored eyes are fixed on those doors. The beauty of his eyes is matched only by the fullness of his lips, and his mahogany colored skin. His slender sinewy figure hides the strength yet developing in his young athletic physique.

Would the audience that had just twenty minutes ago showered him with stomping and whistling filled rounds of applause notice him inconspicuously standing there before them? He had just given the first public performance of his life with a widely popular song, and by hitting notes that would have made Mariah Carey do a double take he brought down the house. Yet most of his peers in the audience were not particularly aware at all that they had just witnessed the birth of a superstar.

The finale music is up; the doors swing open, and like the unbridled waters flowing from a burst dam, a stream of young school kid's spout from the auditorium. A young girl gasps and with ecstatic ardor she calls out hurriedly, "There he is. There's Daniel!"

In an instant a horde of enthusiastic new fans, mostly teenage girls, are buzzing about him like incessant assiduous bees, congratulating him on his performance. He is overwhelmed by the adoration that's being showered upon him, but keeps close to his heart the words his father spoke to him in almost constant reprise. "Be kind, humble, and gracious, when accepting compliments from others. You will win the hearts of those who don't know you, and those who do, will love you even more. "So as he signs his first autographs in the notebooks of his young admirers, he graciously with expressions of deep appreciation thanks those who offer him compliments. When the crowd thins he finds himself alone with a young girl who is importunately doing her utmost to persuade him to work with her dance group. As she follows him down the hall towards his locker he notices a gang of ruffians harassing the schools most renowned pariah, Michael Callan. Michael takes it, to all appearances in stride, with the proverbial you slap one cheek and I'll give you the other attitude. He and his family are members of some religious group that doesn't condone violence or personal retribution of any type, under any circumstances.

Michael's fleetness of foot on the track field usually spares him any threat of physical harm coming into close proximity of him while off it. But today his aggressors succeed in taking him completely by surprise and have cornered him at his locker. One of them moving with the swiftness of a gazelle gives him a sound butt with his hand to the back of his head, while yet another youth snatches his glasses from his nose and hurls them and his books to the ground. „When are ya finally gonna give up that hokey religion Mike? Huh, ...(smack).......huh.........(smack), when? ", asks one.

„Do it today", retorts another boy before kicking him in the rear end. And in a flash they've dispersed and are gone.

Daniel almost feels sorry for him due to the fact that he is filled today with happiness and excitement from his first taste of success. But the unremitting competitiveness between him and Michael quickly re-surfaces and his relent soon fades into an exiguous feeling that Michael a moment ago had been dealt his just desserts. Daniel won't settle for less than the best he can give and imposes a high standard upon himself. He holds the number two position on the track team, but wants the number one spot badly; the spot that Michael Callan indefatigably holds.

Like Michael, Daniel receives his fair share of ridicule from the school jocks, not because of any religious affiliation, but from their viewpoint, for his interest in the sissy sport of singing. He thought his prowess in sports might abate the unceasing malefic mockery from the jocks that never fails to besmirch his self-esteem. Ergo he continually seeks to vie for the number one position on the track team. Daniel is an excellent sprinter, but he nearly always comes in second to Mike Callan who beats him interminably in the sixty and one hundred meter dash, and adding insult to injury, quite often by just a nose. Furthermore, it annoyed Daniel that the track team means very little to Michael compared to his dedication to his religion. Daniel's guided by his ambitious drive and finds it difficult to understand why anyone with talent could allow anything to have priority over career pursuits.

Michael Callan and Daniel Jones attended El Cerrito High School and met for the first time at the age of thirteen while on the school track team in two thousand-fourteen. They were both born in the month of August in the year two thousand-one and were raised in comparatively middle class families in El Cerrito, California where both set of parents painstakingly made a living yet was frugal enough to be considered upper middle class. Their parents went above and beyond the call of duty when making sacrifices for the sake of their children, both of whom are extremely talented, Michael in track and field sports and Daniel in music.

In spite of their nebulous rivalry, Michael in Daniel's eyes is still a track team member, his teammate, and regardless of his ambition Daniel's a bona fide team player. With a sense of team allegiance now fueled by the euphoria of success Daniel walks over to Michael who is in the process of putting himself physically and emotionally back together. As Daniel espies Michael's gestures, he becomes keenly attentive to the sorrow, frustration, and humiliation that left their traces upon Michael's entire physical countenance.

Michael runs his hands through his thick dark brown hair; it more than suffices to restore the clean cut prep. His green eyes unsuccessfully endeavor to suppress the tears that blur his vision and begin to spill over his tawny cheeks. His thin lips, high arched nose, and nickel glasses give him the Clark Kent look of a bookworm which is in sharp contrast to his nimble superman presence on the track field.

Daniel has all to oft bore the brunt of spiteful peers, and as he beholds the aftermath of the maltreat, and feels the impact it has on Michael, genuine sympathy and compassion overtake him.

„Damn", he thought. „They really got to him".

„Are you OK? ", asks Daniel as he puts his hand consolingly upon Michael's shoulder.

„I'm fine", responds Michael.

Displeased and embarrassed that someone is invading his space so soon after the untimely assault Michael brusquely shrugs Daniel's hand from his shoulder.

„Hey man, lighten up. "

„Lighten up? Have you come over here to add to my grief?

And where were YOU when those guys were all over me, huh? " he asks angrily.

Michael kneels to pick up his books, stands up......., takes a deep breath, exhales slowly........., and gathers his composure.

„Hey look, I...I'm sorry, thanks for asking. I'll be alright. "

„Don't let those jealous good for nothings get to you Michael. You've got so much going for you and they can't stand it. I'll see you on the field tomorrow. OK? "

„Yeah, OK. "

„Hey Daniel", Michael adds as Daniel was about to turn to walk away.

„You were great up there on stage. You know, if you keep that up someday you're going to be famous. "

„You really think so? "

„I KNOW SO! "

* * * *

   The world in the year two thousand-fourteen was not altogether different than the world today, only the problems of the world in this twenty-first century year reach multitudinous, as well as magnitudinous proportions. The shameless perfervid greed and corruption of people in positions of power have taken a ruthless toll on the American and global economies, and sends countries, small corporations, businesses, cities, towns, and families, into bankruptcy. Secretly manipulated by an unscrupulous power hungry multi-billionaire Global Elite, (who also hold puissance over governments and the mainstream media corporations) keep their identity and diabolical agenda secret from the general public with misleading and distracting stories, as well as entertainment that headline and dominate the news at every conceivable level. Because of the globalization of the world's economic structure through trade with advanced technology, no country on the face of the earth is spared the inauspicious effects caused by corruption and malfunction in the systems of neighboring or distant countries. Consequently, worldwide the repercussions on justice rendered in the venal judicial systems are profound miscreant conduct. Just as a thief justifies his actions with distorted reasoning, so also does the judiciary in its rendering of injustice at all levels of the system for the sake of yielding revenue for its valetudinarian governments.

   On practically every street corner, in front of every market and convenience store someone can be found asking for pecuniary support. The advancements in technology are rapidly abounding throughout the world and in direct proportion also the decline of moral and ethical standards. Nothing at all about the global economy has the slightest pretext of stability and security. And in less than twelve years it would be pushed to the limit with the impending global devastation left in the wake of the great meteorological cataclysm (brought intentionally to fruition through Geo-Engineering and weather modification) by the Global Elite, and leaves the American economy in a state of total devastation. But for now humanoid robots are in their infancy, yet nonetheless are also wreaking havoc with the global market sending hundred thousands of labor and service related workers into the implausible status of unemployable. As a result the staggering growth of crime due to technology, from identity theft to domestic violence, a rise in the demand for police, criminal investigators, security personnel, and health related services increases significantly. With haste all across-the-board the fabric of the world's society is falling apart at its seams.

Daniel feels the only way he can rise above the wretched condition of the world around him is to use the talent he possesses to catapult him far above it. His father Joseph Henry Jones, better known to his friends as Joe Henry, heard his son one day when he was eight years old singing along to a recording and was amazed by the way his son sang circles around the singer on the original recording. Ever since that day he's encouraged his son's wish to someday become a professional singer. He also advises and guides him, managing jobs for voice over studio gigs. Music creates a special bond between the two of them.

While working a voiceover job at a local studio the topic of operatic singing comes up.

„That's not singing", replies Daniel as he listens in on the conversation from the performers recording booth.

„That's only ya voooh ta hoooh............." in such a strong emphatic operatic soprano voice that the engineer and Joe look at each other stunned and let out a hearty laugh. The audio monitor that connects the engineer's booth to the performer's chamber is suddenly switched off. His father and the engineer begin to converse with each other and their muted chatter seems to Daniel to take an eternity.

„Hey, are you ready to continue or what?", he says impatiently.

„No we've got it. Come in here Daniel please we'd like to talk to you.", is the response from Mark; the recording engineer.

Daniel walks through the two soundproofed doors to the engineer's room where his father and Mark wait to speak to him.

„Your father tells me that you can hit some pretty high notes. I'd like you to listen to a song and then tell me if you think you could sing it. "

Mark presses a button on the mixing console and the first orchestrated notes of the Mozart aria „Queen of the Night" come from the loudspeaker; Daniel begins to frown in disapprobation. But as Birgit Nilsson's voice thunderbolts across the room he leans forward with eyes widened in astonishment. At its finish he replies,

„Wow uh, that wasa.......uh....hoo....wee! ".
„The million dollar question Daniel is do you think you can sing it? "
„Yeah, uh, maybe, but why in the world would I want to sing that? " he
replies.
„This is why. Have a listen to this."
Mark punches a button and out comes a heavy duty back beat and over it
practically the same orchestration heard earlier in the aria. Daniel sits up in his
chair totally perked.
„Hey......, I like that! "
„Good, I'm glad to hear that. Your Dad and I will work out the details. You learn it
and try to give us as close as you can the opera feeling that you gave us while in
the booth, OK?"

    Throughout the following three days Joe Henry negotiates back and forth over
the phone with Mark the terms of the recording agreement; also keeping Mark
posted on Daniels progress with the piece. He knew this project was something
different and very special and he had a sneaking suspicion that if given proper
treatment it would substantially help his son's career. Moreover, he wanted to
insure that the song stay in the clean zone. Mark mentioned adding a rap, and
rap in the yesteryear of twenty-fourteen had taken a turn to using not only
extremely obnoxious language, but also blasphemous expressions, with which
Joe wanted no sharing of the recorded platform with his sons' voice. Daniel in
the meantime goes about learning the aria as just another exercise that'll expand
his musical horizons. He possesses the sui generis talent of accurate vocal
emulation; that leaves barely a trace of audible differentiation from the original
and his, to the listener's ear.

    On the evening of the recording session Mark and Joe are astounded by the
precision of Daniel's autodidactic adeptness in operatic singing. After having
warmed up, he sings the aria practically in one take. When Daniel finished Mark
says to Joe in an undertone,
„We have a hit on our hands if, we can get a bit of steady airplay on this. "
„By God, I believe you're right! Did you hear how he sang that? "
„Yeah, his coloration of tone and emphasis, especially when he hit those
downbeats is phenomenal. Let me hear it again. "
„Daniel we're going to listen to that take again before we call you in. "comes
Mark's voice over Daniel's headset.
„OK"
Their hearts race as they listen again and when the song ended Mark says,
„Thanks Daniel, we've got it. "

* * * *

THE LAST DAYS AND THE GREAT TRIBULATION - THE PAST

THE BIRTH OF GOD'S CHIEF ADVERSARY

In the beginning God created the heavens and the earth or so it is written. We dwell upon the face of the earth, but how well do we know the earth and its true relationship to the heavens? Is there a relationship between heaven and earth? And if there is a heavenly realm; who lives there and what is life like there? **Nehemiah** wrote, „ Blessed be your glorious name, and may it be exalted above all blessing and praise. You alone are God. You made the heavens, even the highest heavens, and all their starry host, the earth and all that is on it, the seas and all that is in them. You give life to everything, and the multitudes of heaven worship you. " In the book of **First Kings** the prophet **Jeremiah** noted, „then hear from heaven, your dwelling place. Forgive and act; deal with each man according to all he does, since you know his heart (for you alone know the hearts of all men)".

There lives in heaven God Almighty and a multitude that worships him, angels that serve and minister to him. As personalities angels have the power to communicate with one another, and the thinking ability with which to glorify and praise God; or not to. The Angels were created by God and his firstborn Son who is the beginning of creation by God. They are also known as sons of God. The angels were individually created long before the earth or man's appearance. For at the founding of the earth together the morning stars joyfully cried out and all the angels shouted for joy. - **Job 38:4-7, John 1:3**

Angels are sometimes referred to as spirits; that which is spirit is invisible to man and powerful. Having invisible spirit bodies, they dwell in the heavens. A peaceful abode must the heavens be, or why is it most people believe that is where good people go after death, and there in heaven only true peace is attainable? Perhaps, it is the physical description of the heavens and God's domain which has been elusively and graphically depicted so often throughout history, or the attributes of its inhabitants which lends to such splendid peaceful living there.

Yet, out of this peaceful domain came an angel that desired the worship from man that belonged solely to God. He was when created, a perfect, righteous creature of God. From a virtuous perfect start, this spirit person deviated into imperfection and degradation. God Almighty expressed it so poignantly when **Ezekiel** recorded His words,

„You were the model of perfection, full of wisdom and perfect in beauty. You were in Eden, the garden of God; every precious stone adorned you: ruby, topaz and emerald, chrysolite, onyx and jasper, sapphire, turquoise and beryl. Your settings and mountings were made of gold; on the day you were created they were prepared.
You were anointed as a guardian cherub, for so I ordained you.
You were on the holy mount of God; you walked among the fiery stones.
You were blameless in your ways from the day you were created till wickedness

was found in you. "- **Ezekiel 28:11-15**

What was the wickedness found in this once perfect angel? One facet of it is his deliberate and calculated concealment of himself to man, starting with the first man, Adam; so that he would receive the deference from him that belonged to his Creator. Adam and his wife Eve; the father and mother of mankind were perfect, created with the unique facility of reason, and were approached and seduced by the angel before they could pass their perfection on to their children. We've all heard the story in some form or another, as it is for many revered as a myth only worthy of being categorized and filed under and along with Santa Claus in its validity, despite the support of Adam and Eve's existence; as recorded also in many of the Greek (New Testament) scriptures. As such, the greatest deception of all time, which began with this angel's rebellion, continues to march on, down to this day.

I ask; how do YOU feel when someone has intentionally deceived you? Think for a minute about it; the anguish you suffer when you're deceived by someone you've trusted, and perhaps even loved. Think about how the distress is compounded when the deception is found to be deliberate, and with malice of intent. It hurts, does it not? Grief such as this never was found in heaven or on earth until this once perfect angel set his heart on obtaining what belonged to his Creator, and subsequently this angel became the father of the lie, and every other deception known to mankind.

His ostensibly humble beginning as Satan the Devil, and God's chief adversary started when he cunningly convinced Eve to be disobedient and partake of the one thing God Almighty asked her and Adam not to touch; namely the fruit from the tree of the knowledge of good and bad.

There were two trees in the middle of the Garden of Eden. One was the tree of life and the other as stated, was the tree of the knowledge of good and evil. Everything upon the earth was at their command. As a symbol of God's sovereign right to rule over them and the universe, they were instructed not to eat the fruit of this tree. Indeed, not a tremendous task; obedience to one law, is all God asked in contrast to, and in return for giving everlasting life and everything upon the earth He created for them. Think of it, in their day there was only one law to uphold for peace and perfection on the earth, instead of the many manmade laws now on the books; most of them providing windows of escape for the greedy and corrupt at heart to take, to the detriment of their fellow man undue advantage. Imagine how easy life would have been if we had been allowed everything as children in return for honoring one rule designated by our parents. Adam and Eve were given perfection and everlasting life, if they would only uphold and preserve God's one law; not to eat of that fruit, no, not even to touch it, for if they did they would surely die.

„Therefore, just as sin entered the world through one man, and death through sin, and in this way death came to all men, "- **Romans 5:12**

How Adam and Eve were confronted with the diabolical scheme of the angel is something that many people truly believe is a fairy tale. The same people, mind you, who emphatically give credence to, and wholeheartedly accept the existence of gods; such as Poseidon, Apollo, Zeus, who purportedly have the power to transmogrify themselves to seduce and subvert mortals. Well, in like manner, the angel used the serpent to deceptively provide Eve with an enticement to take of the fruit. He thus becomes histories' first liar, the father of the lie.

The account in the book of **Genesis** exposes his deceptive plot:
„Now the serpent was more crafty than any of the wild animals the Lord God had made. He said to the woman, „Did God really say, „You must not eat from any tree in the garden"? "
The Woman said to the serpent, „We may eat fruit from the trees in the garden, but God did say, „You must not eat fruit from the tree that is in the middle of the garden, and you must not touch it, or you will die.""
„You will not surely die, "the serpent said to the woman. „For God knows that when you eat of it your eyes will be opened, and you will be like God, knowing good and evil. "

There in the last quoted sentence is found the bait he used; to present Eve with an illusory self-rectification program to the improvement of God's plan for her, her husband, and their offspring (mankind). In aspiring to know as much as God and become Godlike or a Goddess, she chose to judge for herself what is right or wrong instead of yielding to God's right to make that decision for her. In essence and unbeknownst to her the angel successfully persuaded her to have him, instead of God as her Lord and Master in an open rebellion against God Almighty their creator. Eve effectively persuaded Adam to rebel with her when he successively ate the fruit; a rebellion that would dramatically affect all of mankind henceforth, as they had not yet produced any offspring. Thus the initiation of the great deception by the angel was made complete.

When God discovered the rebellious plot; sentences were passed on all three. If you look closely at the account in **Genesis chapter three** take note that when discovered there was no repentance or concession of accountability by Eve or Adam. No, they more or less put the blame the way children often do on someone or something else. Consequently the enjoyment and privilege of everlasting life in the perfect garden were no longer viable options for Adam and Eve.
„"He must not be allowed to reach out his hand and take also from the tree of life and eat, and live forever. "
So the Lord God banished him from the Garden of Eden to work the ground from which he had been taken. After he drove the man out, he placed on the east side of the Garden of Eden cherubim and a flaming sword flashing back and forth to guard the way to the tree of life."

The angel was given an even worse sentence that is to this day on its advanced inevitable course of fulfillment. To the fallen angel God spoke in the first recorded prophecy of the Bible,
„"And I will put enmity between you and the woman, and between your offspring and hers; he will crush your head, and you will strike his heel. ""

Thus in this first prophecy recorded in Genesis, God Almighty revealed that it was his purpose to empower a „seed" to crush Satan and his forces and to prove the rightfulness of His sovereignty. That „seed" came to be Jesus Christ, along with a distinct group of associate rulers.

This was the birth of Satan the Devil whom I shall refer to often as God's Chief Adversary with exception when quoting the Bible. I refer to him as such because he has successfully distorted and concealed his image, identity, purpose, those who work with him and the name Satan the Devil to most of ancient and modern mankind. „And no wonder for Satan himself keeps transforming himself into an angel of light". - **2 Corinthians 11:14**

Yet of extreme pertinence to those living in these last days, the book of Revelation highlights the origin, identity, those who work with him, and purpose of God's chief adversary with the following words. „So down the great dragon was hurled, the original serpent, the one called Devil and Satan, who is misleading the entire inhabited earth; he was hurled down to earth, and his angels were hurled down with him." - **Revelation 12:9**

* * * *

DISPUTE

In the days following the recording session Daniel goes back to his regular routine at school and with the track team. Michael continues to defeat him during training workouts, which in of itself makes friendly interrelations between the two of them nearly impossible. Daniel is however with music becoming increasingly popular locally with the help of his father who makes certain he comes in contact with the finest musicians the San Francisco bay area music scene has to offer. He accomplishes this with the help of twenty-first century low cost cutting-edge audio and visual recording devices that keep a more than sufficient high quality reproduction of his son's talents. Through steady research he secures unerring inside information about the work, achievements, and predilections of each musician he chooses as candidates for musical accompaniment to Daniel. Amiably seasoned declarations of admiration opens the door to conversational exchanges with them, and this nine times out of ten results in their eventually listening and watching Daniel in brilliant performance over the mini-laptop computer he religiously at all times keeps within close proximity.

Joe Henry impresses upon Daniel the prodigious consequence of proficiency to cover more than just the popular hits of the day and introduces him to the world of jazz standards, classical music, and classic popular music. Daniel begins to love these unchartered genres especially when he discovers the impact a musical arrangement has on a song. He learns the art of scat singing by listening closely to Ella Fitzgerald as well as other scat singers with computer tools that decelerate the performance to a tempo that is optimal for him to make a thorough acoustical examination of their technique down to the most infinitesimal nuance. Through osmosis he recreates the performance in actual time embracing the melody with a finesse that was all his own. His father dug out an old CD version of the song „I Will Survive" sung by a male country &

western singer to illustrate to his son the extraordinary effect a style differentiation has on a song. He inspires Daniel to break barriers and never cease to explore the possibilities of a tune before rejecting it. Daniel in his pre-teen years absorbs the instruction from his father like the nourishing waters from an undeviating sluice that sustains the fertile terrain. He responds to the attention, guidance and support his father gives him by sedulously exerting himself knowing that it's in his and their families' best interests. Joe Henry loves good music and having a natural talent for teaching, knows how to make unpopular genres of music educational as well as fun for his son.

Daniel longed for voice lessons, but Joe Henry declined his request. „Voice lessons will only wreck what already comes naturally to you. The piano will make you independent in case you start to write your own songs and arrange your own music. OK?
If you ever experience difficulty singing and begin to lose your voice, then you'll get voice lessons son. ", was Joe Henry's answer.

Daniel's conquests in the local music scene along with reviews in the local news were beginning to inflate his young impressionable ego despite his Dad's advice to keep both feet on the ground. He begins to believe the hype and adulation the press bestows upon him. And it begins to irritate him that he's number one on the track team only during Mike Callan's absence.

One day after having another training victory seized from him once again by Mike, while in the locker room a fellow teammate asks,
„How do you do it Mike? Just when it looks as if one of us is about to whip you, you come up from behind, turn on the juice, and wipe us out. "
„It's not by any power I possess on my own. It's a gift from God. I owe it all to Him. ", acknowledges Michael.
„Oh give us a break. That religious garbage that you devote so much time to is going to send you straight to the poor house if you don't use your God given talent and train for the Olympics.", infuses Daniel.
„You miss far too much training for those religious meetings you attend, and the whole team suffers because of it. "
„My missed training hasn't prevented me from wiping you up off the floor in a match. "
The entire locker room rings with laughter in response to Mike's veridical quip. Daniel infuriated by the humiliating riposte, clad only in a towel charges forward and plunges Michael backwards into his locker, moves in, and with one directly centered gut punch knocks the wind out of him. But like a pivotal reflex, in one swift upward blow Mike's right knee forcefully meets Daniel's groin, and with that both of them exhaustively plummet to the floor.

Yet, in spite of Michael's attempt the very next day to approach Daniel and apologize for his verbal and physical reprisal; from that day forward in Daniel's self-deceptious puerile imagination Mike Callan is his nemesis. Daniel wasn't having any of it and preferred to remain unyieldingly mulish. Under the circumstances Daniel's attitude is understandable from a child's perspective. It wasn't until weeks later that the bruise inflicted by the blow completely healed. The physical injury he sustained made it almost impossible to sing. He believed in the days following their skirmish he'd never be able to sing again. Moreover, Daniel lacked the emotional maturity that Michael acquired during his childhood by means of the Bible based training he received from his parents and their congregation. He failed to realize that Michael's blow wasn't deliberate, and never became aware of the fact having refused to hear Michael out in his apology. He turned, walked away, and subsequently quit the track team a couple of weeks later.

* * * *

   Joe Henry drives up to the curb where Daniel waits for him in front of the school. Daniel has a rehearsal with one of the leading local jazz trios that are featuring him in one of the most prominent jazz clubs in San Francisco over the coming weekend.
   With an upsurged state of moral decline in America, sexual related crimes as well as pedophilia is at an all time high. Daniel has developed into a good-looking young boy, easy bait for a conscienceless pedophile. He is Joe and Ida Jones only son, their only child and they are very concerned to say the least over the persistent widespread news reports on crimes of this nature. To Daniel's chagrin Joe insists that he personally drive him to and from the ever increasing number of rehearsals and events where his attendance is required.

„How was school son? " Joe asks as he put the car into drive.
„Boring as usual, you know, I bet those teachers nev.............", Daniel stops in mid sentence as he hears the indistinct sound of his voice in the background coming from the car's radio.
„What's that? "He asks and with posthaste turns up the volume.
„Hey Dad! That's me! "
„Sh......sh.......shuh", is Joe's response.
They both listen raptly as the car's sound system pumps out a very modern version of Mozart's Queen of the Night interspersed with a very catchy rap. Daniel gets goose bumps listening to the lusciously compelling musical arrangement that passionately caresses the melodic strains of his voice. Joe gets goose bumps for very different reasons as he flirts with the thought that his son's career is about to take off and their lives could quite possibly change forever.

„That was Mozart in the twenty-first century creeping fast up the charts in a song called Kings Night by Damon and Devoreaux D. Jones."
„ Devoreaux D. Jones? Who's that? Daniel asks.
„It's YOU son. "
Joe turns the radio off.
The both of them are thoroughly immersed in contemplative silence as Joe drives to the rehearsal hall.
Upon arriving Joe put the car in park, switches the motor off, turns to his son and

says,

„I want you to be cool at the rehearsal. Don't make any mention of this until I've gotten more info son, OK? I've got some phone calls to make to check out how big or small this radio thing is. If you brag too much and make this bigger than it is, they'll laugh at you later. "

Daniel chuckles and with a ventriloquist's lipped mimic mutters,

„Let 'em laugh. "

Daniel loved jazz, but he hated the downright haughty arrogance most jazz players have towards music that is in any way remotely associated with top forty. He relished the thought of smearing his hit top forty jam all over their avant-garde bread and butter.

„But this IS big Dad, isn't it? You heard him say that the song is creeping fast up the charts. "

„Yeah, I heard him say it. ", replies Joe.

"But just let your old man check it out to be sure. Do this for me OK? I'll know a lot more real soon. Then you can talk about it Saturday Night all you want. "

Daniel exasperatingly sighs.

„OK Dad, I'll keep quiet for now. "

Thanks D. Now go in there and knock their socks off. "

Daniel springs from the car and bolts towards the door, then stops short of the door when he suddenly realizes that his father had just called him by his new name; and he liked it. He liked it a lot! He turns around to wave good-bye, but Joe's already busy talking to someone on his cell phone.

When he enters the rehearsal hall the band was on a break. He had stepped right into the middle of a conversation. After they all greet him the bass player continues to tell the others about how his daughter is listening non-stop to some rap song set to Mozart. He goes on to say,

„In this day and age I'm glad she's listenin' to classical music even if it is fused with rap. "

That remark now made it ever so easy for Daniel to keep the promise he had just made his Dad.

Daniel had a big secret and was all smiles inside.

Within a week Daniel begins to take to his new name, but his friends as well as his fans begin to call him D.

* * * *

METAMORPHOSE

D. Jones arrives on the set in the financial district of New York City at Federal Hall punctually at three a.m. with his Uncle Benjamin Jones who doubles as his driver and bodyguard for the trip. To actually work on the set of a major motion picture was everything and more than he had imagined it would be. There's a lot of bustle on the set, but upon his arrival he's promptly met and greeted by the casting director of the film.

She proceeds to give him a small tour of the location set and then escorts him to his trailer. D is awestruck and barely hears a word she says as he watches the crews prep the great white steps of the Federal Hall Building for the days scheduled shoot. The statue of George Washington has been removed leaving an untenanted pedestal. The scene calls for D and a gospel choir to sing the song "Oh Happy Day" on location at Federal Hall at sunrise. The story of the film is about a young man who makes his way to the top of Wall Street. The scene with D is a daydream sequence following the lead characters first big windfall on his way to the top.

D was offered a cameo role in the film because he is a rising star in the music industry; hence a very marketable parallel befitting the film's story line. D's agent was not at all impressed by the idea. He wanted to reserve D's talents for something bigger that would impart a more striking debut for him into the world of films. But when D received word of the offer and that it was a cameo role with the lead vocal on "Oh Happy Day" he became adamant about accepting the part. Even if the film became a flop at the box office, he was certain it would be worth it for the sheer pleasure of rubbing elbows with the stars of the film and the experience of having a part in a major motion picture.

The primary shooting schedule for the film was complete, but the film's director, John McBride had recently seen D's latest music video "On The Run" and was so impressed by the energy of D's performance, it inspired an idea to make him part of his film with a cameo role in a daydream sequence. He presented his concept of D's part to the film's producer who with very little persuasion was very impressed with the idea, and proceeded immediately to contact D's agent with the proposal and an offer. With lots of hesitation and negotiation on the part of his agent the deal was settled. The only stipulation was that they get all they needed from D on film in one day's work and have him back on a plane to Los Angeles directly after the shoot. One other proviso on D's part was that he would arrive in New York a day early in order to indulge in some sightseeing.

"I've just got to see the view of Manhattan Island from the top of the Empire State Building." he said with youthful exuberance.

"What good is all of the work if I can't enjoy the fruits of my labor." he adds jokingly knowing that he in every way loved his work.

Those listening knew all too well that those were not D's words, but those of Ida Jones his Mom. She is a firm believer that all work and no play would eventually make her son very unhappy. She also insisted that he stay at a Hotel in New Jersey.

"New York City is a hot bed, a target area, and I don't want him staying at a hotel in the City." she demanded regarding the film project.

The production company booked him a Suite at the Hilton Gateway Hotel in Newark, New Jersey. Ben has a room within the suite with him. D's at a phase in his career where he could be easily recognized while out in public and that is why Ben, Joe's brother is always with him on business. D has a couple of disguises though. His favorite is putting on the nerd look complete with big glasses and protruding false teeth, the kind that Jerry Lewis wore in his slapstick roles. If any young fans come across as if they're about to become awestruck, he flashes his ghastly fake choppers, and they instantaneously in grimace lose interest.

After enjoying a very exciting day with Ben seeing the sights of New York; the Apollo Theatre, the Met, Times Square, Central Park, and the Empire State Building, Ben with a great deal of persuasion gets him back to Newark in time for a shower, room service dinner, a quick call to Joe and Ida, and into bed by 9:00 pm.
"You've got an early shoot tomorrow young man now lights out. "
"Yes Dad," says D a bit begrudgingly.
As he drifts off to sleep he ponders all the things and places he had seen, and thought what a wonderful world. Someday I'm going to live in New York City.
Back in his trailer D waits in costume; a red cape like coat, ruffled white shirt with a buttoned down vest, form-fitting black trousers, and black boots, all of the finest design and material was what the costume designer came up with for him to wear in the film. The allure of New York City still danced in his mind and heart. In the background on a tiny, but very high powered recording device that's small enough to fit in a backpack, the pre-recorded track for the film's scene plays over and over again in his trailer. This is his way of psyching himself up for the shoot.
While getting the last touches put on his make-up the film's director John McBride knocks and then enters D's trailer.
"How are you D?" he asks.
"Just fine John and ready to do it. How far along are we?"
John looks at his watch.
"Almost there, sunrise in an hour. "
"Hey Beth how much more time do you need with him?"
"Two minutes" she replies.
"Come on out when you're ready D."
"OK, see you there."
As D leaves his trailer and begins to approach the set he is greeted by cheers, screams, and applause from the fifty choral singers dressed in radiantly deep blue choral gowns awaiting his arrival standing on the steps of Federal Hall. As the applause begins to fade John speaks through the megaphone.
"OK, before the sun comes up for the shoot lets run a rehearsal of the number." Everyone takes there places and silence sets in. The faint sound of birds chirping and an emergency vehicle siren in the distance are the only audible sounds.
"Here we go aaand............. Action." says John.
A close-up on D's bowed head singing a cappella the opening lines of „Oh Happy Day" introduces the scene. He proceeds in song as the camera gradually zooms out to reveal D solitarily standing on George Washington's vacated pedestal. An elaborate hydraulic lift for dramatic effect and height has been added to the pedestal, which D stands upon in exact pose of the removed statue, with the mammoth staircase and the majestic pillars of Federal Hall as

his backdrop. On „He taught me how....." the soundtrack gives the stentorian call as the supporting cast of choral singers flow in harmonious progression from the flanking portals of the building into choral formation at the top levels of the stairway leaving enough space to the center portal of the building for the forthcoming action. To D's surprise the choir joins the pre-recorded choir of the soundtrack in song, imparting an ancillary uplift of interactive energy he unhesitatingly fuses in exuberant rounds of call and response exchange that renders an exceptional performance for the camera. To preserve the driving catalysis the sound engineer pumps up the volume of the soundtrack that is imperil of fading to a drone amidst the resplendent vocal prowess of the choir.

Three of the five cameras on cranes in sweeping motion billow and swerve to the pulsating cadence of the music. Suddenly D leaps with the grace of a seasoned ballet dancer from the pedestal, cape coat flowing in the wind behind him and lands light-footed as he begins to dance up the staircase of Federal Hall with Fred Astairean panache. Unexpectedly the star of the film enters through the center portal and joins D cleverly complementing D's steps, bolstering the magic of the moment with the endearing comedic klutz of his character. He and D now begin to ingeniously improvise the scene in a poetically aesthetic mellifluous collaboration. Passersby on the street are now starting to converge, closing in on the barrier around the set to get close enough to see an amazing show of lights, camera, and action. A fervent climax ensues with the last musical crescendo that enchants those watching as they become aware that they are witnessing entertainment history in the making. With the last choral refrain of the song the listener is left in ebullience; musically taken to the height of Mount Everest and subsequently tenderly reposed in a serene and peaceful valley by the quiet banks of a still river.

"Cut and print it." shouts John enthusiastically through the megaphone.
"That was beautiful and as you can see the sun rose during the last take ladies and gentlemen.
But we're going to do it again until you get it right, OK?' John light-heartedly decrees.
Laughter from the cast and onlookers ensue his sally.
"Take five to freshen up.", says the assistant director.

Beth runs over to D with a fresh white towel and make-up kit in hand.
"Hello I'm Jason Dupree" says the star of the film a bit out of breath as he extends his hand to D.
D reaches out and greets him with a firm handshake.
"Pleasure to meet you Jason."
"The pleasure's mine. Where in the world did you learn to move like that?" he asks.
"It just comes naturally." is D's response.
"Well, He blessed you abundantly. I'll see you back here in ten.
They'll kill us if we stand here flapping our jaws too long."
"See you Jason."

With that Beth takes her cue and begins hurriedly to refresh D's make-up. The clock was ticking.

After another series of short takes John knew he had the feature film debut performance of a rising star in his possession. The crews begin to strike the location set-up at lightning speed and had evacuated the vicinity of Federal Hall in less than an hour. The set is broken before the onslaught march of the Wall-Streeters begins in earnest to pound its pavements. All that was left on the site is but an elusive remembrance of film-making magic. A remembrance now documented on film by John McBride and Ben Jones. Yes, Ben was also busy during the most critical moments of D's career. With his Camcorder he caught the special moment when Jason Dupree approached him in introduction, and when D walked onto the set and was greeted with exultant applause from the choir, crew, and spectators behind the barriers. He captured all of it. He knew the import of keeping a well documented, behind the scenes record on the life of his nephew.

Most of the crew was flying back that morning from either JFK or Newark International Airport. John McBride put his assistant director on a plane with the day's daily footage. He has decided since he had wrapped up the shooting of his film with a resounding finale he would celebrate and stay in New York another day and enjoy as D so aptly put it during a phone conversation "the fruits of his labor".

D is in a state of euphoric languor as Ben drives them in the rental car to Newark International Airport to catch an eleven-thirty flight to Los Angeles.
"It went well didn't it Ben?" D asks.
"It went very well D, your folks are gonna be real proud of you."
"Are you Ben?"
Ben stretches out his hand and places it on D's shoulder and says,
"I'm awfully proud of you! You'll shine like a diamond when that film is released. Hey, I've got something to show you once were in the air that I think you'll like."
"What, what is it?" D asks with perked inquisitiveness.
"It's a surprise now, you'll see soon enough." Ben says as he smiles.

They arrive at the airport and Ben drives up to the departure level and stops where a man and a woman are awaiting their arrival; one to take the rental-car and the other to take their luggage, and are then on their way through the security check point before entering the VIP lounge.

Once on board an overwhelming sense of well-being overcomes Ben. As if he and D were somehow now out of harm's way. When you've been in the security business as long as he has you develop a sixth sense regarding the safety of the environment one happens to be in at any given time. Having spent time in quieter, calmer parts of the world including an extended time in the smaller cities of Europe, he has on occasion said there is no other place in the world like New York City where one must constantly be on guard.

As the plane takes off his tension eases as he quickly dispels the momentary sensation of danger, chalking it up to no more than his natural vigilant demeanor for the world of New York City. He's always enjoyed the ascent of an airplane, especially when leaving any big city. It was like the soothing lull of a good rocking chair. D has his most favored position; the window seat and Ben his, which was the aisle seat where he could stretch his long legs, much to the disfavor of the flight attendants who when in a hurry would sometimes stumble over his feet.

He begins to drift into a state of half sleep as the jet slowly approaches its cruising altitude, when suddenly from the back of the cabin comes an ear piercing scream from a woman, thereafter followed by moans and cries from other passengers. Ben looks back, but his attention is also at once, keen to the man sitting two rows in front of him say to his wife,

"Honey did you see that! "

Annoyingly awakened she replies in an apathetic tone, "What is it?"

Ben's first instinct is with D. He directs his attention to him. D is staring out of the window, eyes widened, jaw dropped.

D nervously gulps and asks Ben,

"Where's the Camcorder?"

"In your backpack, why?"

D scurries with lightning speed, takes the camera out of the backpack from beneath the seat in front of him, and aims out the window and begins to record. Ben instantaneously unbuckles his seat belt and peers over D's shoulder out the window onto the island of Manhattan.

„I'll be damned. ", he says.

It is a clear sunny day without a cloud in the sky, except for a cloud that is slowly rising out of a fulminate conflagration near lower Manhattan. In a matter of seconds an explosion of blinding incandescence bolts across the sky and in a split second its presence seems to devour the entire firmament in its luminance; yet, roughly figured to be, as seen from their bird's eye view, another thirty to forty blocks north of the first cloud of smoke still hovering over the Manhattan peninsula. An explosion synonymous to those demonstrated in documentary films about nuclear holocausts, albeit of subordinate magnitude. The successive dark dense circular cloud of smoke and dust now expands outward, and mushrooms upward towards the heavens with extraordinary speed in its ominous ascent. It was indeed a dreadful spectacle, though anomalously it would be considered beautiful in its subsequent iridescence; if you had not at this very moment become personally acquainted with that which spells unprecedented devastation.

In the cabin the wailing and plangent cries could be heard for the fate of friends and loved ones left behind with whom some on board the aircraft had just said good-bye to at the airport and in the city. And then in a flash another explosion of light radiates from the upper part of Manhattan Island; by a rough estimate Ben places it in the seventy or eighties blocks.

Shrieks of "Oh my God", echo throughout the cabin as practically every passenger scrambles to the right side of the plane in an attempt to get a glimpse of the catastrophe unfolding below. The plane suddenly makes a sharp downward plunge to the right as screams from the passengers entrench the cabin.

The accompanying tone of the fasten seat belt sign knells in succession, yet ineffectively bringing the passengers back to their assigned seats, and at once

the Captain's voice can be heard over the PA saying,
"Ladies and Gentlemen, please remain in your seats. We are all extremely alarmed by what's happening, but we will be in danger of crashing if the bulk weight of the aircraft continues to be placed on the right side of the aircraft. Please return to your seats and we will switch on the fuselage video cameras to the monitors for you to see what is happening on Manhattan as soon as possible. Please return to your seats and fasten your seat belts. Be advised that we owe it to other flights that have taken off to leave this airspace as soon as possible." The flight attendants at once go to work assisting passengers to their seats as they consolingly reiterate the words spoken by the Captain a moment ago.

D's hands are glued in a state of shock to the camera as the view of Manhattan slowly fades in the distance.
"Let go of the camera D......, c'mon D, c'mon let go." pleads Ben as he now circumspectly prize the camera from his hands.

D sank his head against the window as the teardrops fell from his disbelieving eyes. Ben lifts the armrest and puts his arm around D and his hand gently across his forehead in an effort to shield his eyes from the disaster looming over the horizon on the other side of the airplane window. In startled reflex D breaks free to look back and see in the distance the three inauspicious clouds progressively enmesh. Ben pulls him back to him and D's head involuntarily lolls against his chest. Amidst the din of the passenger's ineludible plaints, D silently wept.

* * * *

CHAPTER TWO

THE LAST DAYS AND THE GREAT TRIBULATION - PRESENT

GOD'S CHIEF ADVERSARY'S MARCH THROUGH MANKIND'S HISTORY

„On this account be glad, YOU heavens and YOU who reside in them! Woe for the earth and for the sea, because the Devil has come down to YOU, having great anger, knowing he has a short period of time. "- **Revelation 12:12**
But for mankind who through generation after generation come and go in death, it appears that this short period of time is equivalent to eternity; to the extent, that most of mankind no longer believes that any real change of biblical significance will ever occur here on earth. To quote a well known phrase and common belief, it would seem that „ nothing is certain in life but death and taxes". Death, taxes, and evil have been amongst us for as long as man's secular collective recorded history; yet life as we know it still continues and will continue as „it always has", is the popular presumption.
-2 Peter 3: 3, 4

How can God's chief adversary and his angels turned into demons live among us and yet we are unable to see them? Consider for a moment that we are unable to visually see the wind. Does that make it a lesser reality because it is invisible to the human eye? Nevertheless, you know it exists when you feel its coolness or warmth brush across your skin, or when you have seen or felt its devastating effects as experienced in a hurricane. Its impact can be subtly and at times severely felt. In much the same way we feel the effect and see the result of the powerful presence of God's chief adversary and his agents, spirit and human, here on earth.

Satan and his spirit creatures as regards our physical eyesight, which have been hurled down from heaven now dwell in the invisible realm here in the vicinity of the earth. They profoundly influence the very fiber of the spirit or attitude of the world we live in. This spirit's fundamental pre-eminence is embedded in the superficially sound premise that man solely is capable of solving his problems, achieved only, within the bounds of freedom of his rulership over himself. To give ample credence to this equivocal presupposition, Satan the Devil, and expressly his name is kept with any degree of serious credibility ascribed to it, as far from the realm of reality in the minds of the masses as possible; moreover also the name, Jehovah, the true name and identity of God Almighty his enemy as represented with the Hebraic Tetragrammaton יהוה.

„the whole world is lying in the power of the wicked one." - First John 5:19

Jesus did not dispute the issue that Satan held power here on earth, or that the kingdoms of the world were within his power to give. Evident in the account recorded at **Matthew chapter four, verses eight to eleven**:
„Again the Devil took him along to an unusually high mountain, and showed him all the kingdoms of the world and their glory, and he said to him: „All these things I will give you if you fall down and do an act of worship to me. " Then Jesus said to him: „Go away, Satan! For it is written, „It is Jehovah your God you must worship, and it is to him alone you must render sacred service." Then the devil left him, and, look! Angels came and began to minister to him. "
If Satan had not these governments within his power, wouldn't Jesus have told him so?

„ in which you at one time walked according to the system of things of this world, according to the ruler of the authority of the AIR, the spirit that now operates in the sons of disobedience." - Ephesians 2:2

The attitude that permeates the spirit of the world is clearly conspicuous. It is the attitude God's adversary has held since the beginning of his birth in the Garden of Eden. All one need do is look around and observe the manifestation of human life on earth as expressed through mainstream communications. It exalts the created objects of man, placing little or no value on nature or the things created by God, even going as far as denying that God had a role in creation. These maniifestations are sometimes conveyed explicitly, yet more often subtly; discernable in advertisements, the net, films, media, or any form of artistic, scientific, and political expressions through the world's leading media institutions. I ask you, is it greed, corruption, jealousy, violence, arrogance, pride, sorcery, selfishness, pleasure, war, and licentiousness; or is it that which is in direct opposition to these, as example love, joy, peace, patience, kindness, goodness, faithfulness, gentleness, self-control the news that is most often reported for the sake of entertainment and profit in major headlines throughout the world? Of course, there are those who feel that bad news is good news. These however are the ones, the human element who are influenced by, and willingly contribute to this spirit, and share, whether they know it or not, the same frame of mind as their lord and master, God's chief adversary.

„If, now, the good news we declare is in fact veiled, it is veiled among those who are perishing, among whom the god of this system of things has blinded the minds of the unbelievers, that the illumination of the glorious good news about the Christ, who is the image of God, might not shine through." - 2 Corinthians 4: 3, 4

God's chief adversary's purpose is to conceal the accurate knowledge of the good news proclaimed in the Bible from mankind, and to break the integrity of those who have found it, in order that they may not benefit from it, and perish with him. It is bad news for him when he is exposed and people see him and his agents as they really are. For they then no longer in blindness willingly follow him into his inevitable complete demise. They abandon him in a one-hundred and eighty degree tour de force egress. And as unbelievable as it may seem to humans, Satan's time left here on earth, especially from the perspective of those who dwell in heaven, is ephemeral.

„But do not ignore this one fact, beloved, that with the lord one day is as a thousand years, and a thousand years as one day. The Lord is not slow about his promise as some count slowness, but is forbearing toward you, not wishing that any should perish, but that all should reach repentance.......But according to his promise we wait for new heavens and a new earth in which righteousness dwells. - 2 Peter 3: 8-13

„Now there is a judging of this world, now the ruler of this world

will be cast out. "- John 12: 31

God's chief adversary and his band of angels were ousted from the heavens. Their time in heaven came to an abrupt end, just as it will here on earth. Their deceit and rebellious attitude no longer was tolerated in the heavenly realm. God Almighty's will, with great rejoicing of all who reside in heaven has taken place. The GOOD NEWS is that the earth and its surviving inhabitants are next in line for such ginormous jubilation. Unimaginably free from all of God's chief adversary's subversive elements that exist and prevail in the world as we now know it today.

„Thy kingdom come, Thy will be done, on **earth** as it is in heaven. "

* * * *

AFTERMATH

„We're visiting our neighbors to ask them if they would like to know more about God's provi.................."

„I don't believe in God. And besides religion is only an opiate for the people. ", replies the man before slamming the door in Mike Callan's face.

Mike stands there a bit dumbfounded by the abruptness of the man's maneuver, but soon accepts the rejection as he walks towards the sidewalk away from the man's door.

„Rather slow morning isn't it Mike. ", says Gary, the young man who is accompanying Mike today in his door to door field service.

"We've been out here almost two hours and aside from the lady who hurriedly took a brochure there's been nobody who's shown even a remote interest in God or the Bible. Why don't we take a break and have some coffee, then put in another hour before we call it a day. "

„Sounds good to me, I sure could use a break and some coffee. " replies Mike.

When they arrive at the local coffee shop they find a spot and within a short while they are waited upon by a Humanoid who proceeds to take their order for coffee and Danish pastry.

„When were you baptized? ", asks Gary.

„In two thousand-eleven, and you? "

„Two thousand-nine. I hear you're pretty good in track and field. Your leading the school team to victory made headlines. I know its three years down the line, but have you considered entering the Olympics in twenty-twenty? "

„I thought about it, but as you probably can guess my parents are against it. They feel it would be an unwise investment of my time and energy. They say that if I won the Olympics, two years later, my accomplishments would be forgotten even if I continued to win at other competitions afterwards.", says Mike and then pauses.

„And you know something Gary, I think they're right, that's why I'll more than likely not pursue it. To compete in the Olympics you have to eat, drink, and sleep competition. You've gotta be consumed with winning. And I'm not at all. "

„You know most celebrities are here today and gone tomorrow. Only those who have an extraordinarily bad reputation by doing the outrageous or something illegal get publicity and thereby are kept in the minds of the public today.", adds Gary.

„Yeah, you know, that, that's true. And what a way to be kept in mind for the adoration of the populace. It's no wonder that an aversion to religion is so prevalent in the world today. But you know Gary, even as frustrating as it was these past two hours in the field, we've had the opportunity to get to know each other better."

Gary smiles.

"You know Gary, the thing that brings me the most joy is finding someone who shows interest and eventually accepts the truth. And if that one continues to stick with it you know you have helped save a life. I have more or less decided that is the work I want to do on as much of a full time basis as possible. When I look around and see what the world has come to I really feel as my parent's do, that we are in the final milliseconds of the last days. "

"I agree. ", says Gary.

„The great majority of people today feel that religion is the cause of most of the worlds conflicts which is a sure sign that we are awfully close."

    „Oh hey, I almost forgot, I promised my mom I would call her when we break. " Mike takes the cell phone out of his bag and turns it on. He usually shuts it off while working door to door to avoid unnecessary interruptions. He hits the quick dial and his Mom answers,

„Hello. "

„Hi Mom, we're taking a break and about to go back in.........."

„Oh Michael I'm so glad it's you. Come home now! Something terrible has happened in New York, a nuclear explosion of some kind. The country has been put on red alert. Please come home immediately. ", she implores.

„OK, OK, I'm on my way. "

Michael pauses.

„What's up? "

„Something's happened in New York, a nuclear explosion or something. Maybe we can get news of it on the radio in the car. We should both head home now. My mom says the country's on red alert. "

„Oh my God!!! ", comes the cry of a woman's voice from the kitchen area followed by her emotional wailing in Spanish.

A man appears from the kitchen area and announces,

„Excuse me please, excuse me everyone, we've just gotten news that New York City has come under nuclear attack. "

    The Spanish proprietor of the coffee shop prefers usually not to have the wide screen television on unless there's a major sports or music event happening that would attract patrons. But now he clicks the remote and on the screen appears an image that would be repeated over the next days, weeks, and months. An aerial view from a helicopter flying over the east side of the Hudson River of a mushroom smoke cloud. Then a blinding fulgent explosion followed by an array of lucent white and colored light. The circular circumscribed area of the explosion at the base, and then the mushrooming upward into a fuliginous cloud ascending directly towards the helicopter's camera. Suddenly the cameraman shouts,

„ Jim, get us the hell outta here", and before he could finish the sentence the pilot at full tilt veers left and away from the impending danger.

   The images sufficed before Michael's Mom's plea to come home echoes again in his mind. He put the money on the table for his and Gary's coffee and pastry and in a flash they are out the door.

   There's a bitter-sweet silence between them as they walk back to the Kingdom Hall to get their cars and drive home. They witness firsthand the irrepressible fear reflected in the faces of people they see on the streets in a hurry to get home. Everything and everyone ethereally proceeds in slow motion, because despite their hurried pace, not a soul, so it seems could reach their home soon enough. Then suddenly out of the clear blue sky comes the shrill sound of the emergency warning system's sirens.

   When Mike and Gary arrive at the parking lot of the Kingdom Hall, before parting they both look at each other and nod. And as their eyes meet, their eyes convey the one single thought that they both share.

„THIS may very well be the beginning of it. "

* * * *

   The entire country burst into panic on that day they nuked Manhattan Island. Everything shut down and people fled in mass to their homes. And if your house had a basement, it was there you sought refuge. It was a day of great fear and widespread angst. The question written on the face of every American was: Will the next one strike close to a neighboring big city, or my town? Within an hour of the attack it was practically impossible anywhere in the country to make a cell phone call; and if you did get through the call was more than likely shortly thereafter mysteriously cut off. Everything was jammed from the internet to major roadways. Everyone, everywhere in America hastily headed home. All, except those who lived in the New York City region. Due to the presumed threat of radio activity they were fleeing as far away from the vicinity of Manhattan as possible. The thoroughfares leading into New York City were now diverted for greater outbound traffic flow.

   The only objects that move into the city are the RECS; the abbreviated form for the Roving Eye Camera Systems. RECS have become the staple for live coverage over the past five years by journalists for visual propinquity to a breaking news scene free from the obtrusive presence of a cameraman or news team. They are operated by a camera technician from inside of a Newsmobile, with the reporter at a safe distance away from the locus. The RECS are capable of procuring an unencumbered panorama of a newsworthy event.

They have the capacity to hover and move with considerable agility and speed across the longitudinal and latitudinal plane. In addition their new remote control technology made them extremely maneuverable, capable of being remotely piloted up to a distance of one hundred and fifty miles. The RECS are also equipped with extremely powerful high resolution zoom lenses.

The RECS are now the eyes of America that news teams send in by droves to record the devastating aftermath in New York City. Within two hours the first horrifying pictures begin to pour into the networks; images of landmarks and tall buildings which are now only a semblance of their former glory. Some buildings are still ablaze from the nuclear fire. Buildings gutted out by the rush of the atomic wind; dust and darkness. But most shocking and abhorrent are the images of survivors whose decorticate bodies haphazardly dawdle seeking succor within the desolate ruin.

The President makes a live televised address to the American people from an undisclosed location in an attempt to relieve the panic which has spread from coast to coast. He austerely proclaims the greatness of America, his deep sympathy for the victims and their families, and assures the American people that they will find those responsible and bring them to justice.

Flights to La Guardia and JFK that departed before the catastrophe hit are diverted to airports well outside of New York State, while all other flights have been cancelled. Within the following three and a half hours airspace in America is trafficless. Within four hours the streets of America are deserted as most people in the country and around the world are at home or have hunkered down, eyes glued to their television and pc screens.

* * * *

The FBI meets D's flight when it lands at the Los Angeles International Airport. The airport is a madhouse inundated with reporters, security people, and the FBI. When D and Bens aircraft lands and has parked at the gate several men in dark suits come on board. Two of them head immediately to the cockpit. The others begin interviewing the flight attendants. It wasn't long before the chief Stewardess announces,
„Ladies and Gentlemen due to a national red alert security state, we ask that you remain seated until the FBI has completed a walkthrough of the aircraft. "
Heavy sighs and complaints is the collective response from the passengers.
„This shouldn't take more than ten to fifteen minutes", she continues.
„So please let us give the FBI our full cooperation while they perform their duties which are in the interest of our national security and safety. "

More FBI agents appear and begin walking single file through the aisles in groups of three. The first agent is recording with a hand held camera and proceeding at a snail's pace as he receives orders from the other two. When they were finished they leave the aircraft as swiftly as they boarded.

D and Ben are among the first ones off the aircraft and are met by Joe and Ida who both embrace D and are filled with tears of joy upon catching sight of him. They weren't able to reach Ida and Joe from the aircraft by cell phone. The news must have spread like wildfire because all lines within minutes were jammed.

„Oh baby, my baby you're alright, thank God, thank God! ", rejoices Ida as she holds D in her arms. Her tears are indomitable as she's beside herself with joy. Within seconds the paparazzi are upon them and the first shots of professional and non-professional photographers are being taken of the four of them. The jubilant cries of assuagement ring throughout gate twenty-two as the passengers one by one appear through the jet way, as visual contact is made by those who meet their loved ones who are aboard flight twelve-fifteen from Newark.
„Let's get out of here." says Ben.
„Take him out of here. I'll get the bags. "
As they walk away Ida's weeping all but vanquishes to a pule against the joyously resounding ebb and tide of confluence, there at gate twenty-two.

* * * *

FAME

One year later, the tragedy that brought devastating upheaval for most New Yorkers, delivered Devoreaux D. Jones the dawn of a string of career fortune. As with many films when the star of the film dies, the film often reaps unexpected financial success. The success of „All Or Nothing" was astronomical. Jason Dupree the star of the film lost his life; with him John McBride the film's director, along with a dozen others of the film crew who remained in New York City on that tragic day. The film was according to the critics as great a film as its record breaking box office success. It became the epitome of nostalgia as it gave the world its last glimpse of Old New York City. Movie goers lachrymosely exited the theatres deeply moved by the comedic tragedy of the films story line that only augmented the reality of the world's imposed farewell to Old New York City.

Images of D are everywhere; his music, videos, television appearances air around the clock. His popularity increases not only for his performance in the film but because he's now a poster board survivor of a national catastrophe. D however begins to set tight restrictions on his agent with respect the amount of public performance tour bookings, opting to negotiate substantial royalties for his recording, television, and film work. Getting out of New York by the skin of his teeth leaves a psychological scar that makes him disinclined to travel. Recurrent nightmares of being trapped on Wall Street; caught in the holocaust fire haunts his usually peaceful sleep. Fame came with a price.

Despite a year of investigation the FBI and its affiliates are still purportedly clueless as to the identity of the perpetrators of the attack on New York City. Allegedly those responsible martyred themselves as well as obliterating any trace of significant evidence in the nuclear fire. The U.S. government though wants blood, but because of the botched efforts in the last military efforts against Iraq and Afghanistan, the U.N. which over the past year has become more powerful, remains resolute that no action be taken without a definitive smoking gun.
Rumor has it that some fanatical religious groups in the Middle East, in particular

in Iran are responsible for the attack. They're first and foremost suspect because their populaces a r e outspokenly unsympathetic to the American tragedy. Their perspective being America has justifiably reaped what it has sown, especially so with the unnecessary bombing of Japan during the Second World War, as well for the many wars it has waged in its history upon foreign soil. Thus an ever increasing disparagement for religion has taken root in America, and is rapidly gaining worldwide momentum. The movement in actuality is led secretly by the now multi-triillionaire Global Elite whose purpose at this stage of their agenda is to ban the practice of organized religion worldwide. Many renowned professionals from various vocations have conducted extensive research on the history of the Global Elite, comparing and making analysis from the traces of evidence left behind in the New York Nuke and infer that the Global Elite are responsible for the nuking of New York City. And because they are relentless in voicing their findings, an all out campaign to besmirch their reputations has taken place the likes of which would make the McCarthy era in comparison look like a picnic. These professionals conclude that the Global Elite applied once again the principle of "Problem, Reaction, Solution" also executed by the Roman Emperors Diocletian and Nero to achieve that same goal within their agenda. Based on the premise that religion is the fountainhead of conflicts and wars, as well as the enemy of civil rights; they declare it needs to be expunged from the world. Since the attack on New York City, free world countries outside of the United States perceive that they were now more vulnerable than ever to nuclear attack. The world is now ardently resolved to reach a solution to the international security quandary and become swept away in the mounting fervency to eradicate religion.

A very popular television program called „The Curse God and Live Show" is gaining widespread success around the world. In two thousand-seventeen television by way of the internet turns global. Every television station in the world is internet accessible. People are fascinated by this unprecedented new show that pokes fun at anything and everything associated with religion. The writers research a wide variety of religions; their customs, dogmas, beliefs, and present them in comedy routines, music videos, and spoofed news events. The show's success is based on sacrilegious shock and awe.

Damon Marques, the rap artist on D's debut recording of "Kings Night" is a regular cast member of the show. Damon's a pint-sized young man standing five feet, eight inches tall, and weighs in at one hundred and thirty-five pounds. His hair is dyed golden.
„Not blond, not yella, but Gooooolden", he tells his hairdresser.
He frequently has patches at the crown and in the back of his full head of hair of red and purple coloration. His skin is a rich deep cocoa brown. He has an eye and natural talent for combining hues that augment his skin tone. His eyes are small and yield to his proud full African American broad nose that complements his round sumptuous lips. He has the look of an African Prince, but loves to talk like a drunken sailor. He used both his handsome looks and his gift for gab to get the attention of the producers of the „Curse God Show". He has an innate talent for emulation; anyone inclusive of their vernacular speech pattern. With his friends he speaks by choice mostly Afro-American Ebonics.

Damon's a ladies' man. He loves being in the company of women and even with his diminutive figure he usually gets any girl he wants. His counterpart on the "Kings Knight" recording D, is swarmed by girls, but D is driven by sheer ambition and is naturally shy off stage with anyone at first encounter. It's difficult for D to know whether the girls like him for himself or because of his money and fame. Damon on the other hand doesn't care. When Damon suggests to the „Curse God Show" producers that they get D Jones to appear on the show they adamantly and unanimously say,

„No. His music is too goody two shoes for our program. Besides the motto of our show is if you don't curse you don't belong on this show."

„Besides Devoreaux D. Jones is a class act. Look at the places he plays. Even the opera buffs love him. No, no, no, we are sleaze; p r o u d, pure, and exclusively."

But Damon is recalcitrant and determined to break their resolve. He knew that re-uniting with his first recording partner would break new ground for the show because of D's international fame. It would also add some high class glister to his career in re-uniting onstage in front of the camera with D again. He enjoyed the time he spent with D while they were on the road together promoting their first single. They got along famously onstage and off. Damon was in awe of D's raw musical talent and D was taken aback by Damon's witty straightforward and carefree attitude.

* * * *

MICHAEL CALLAN

Michael Callan left all thoughts of a career in sports far behind him after the nuclear attack on New York City. The truth of the Bible engenders a love for God's word that reaches the depths of his heart and wakens in him an unmitigated desire to do as Jesus commanded:

„Go therefore and make disciples of people of all the nations, baptizing them in the name of the Father and of the Son and of the holy spirit, teaching them to observe all the things I have commanded YOU. And, look! I am with YOU all the days until the conclusion of the system of things." - **Matthew 28:19, 20**

Michael pursues this work with zeal recognizing that the history of mankind has reached the periphery of the foretold last days. The inevitable finale of man ruled government everywhere is about to become irrevocable history. With its collective truculent spirit, the world is rapidly approaching the great tribulation, the antecedent of Armageddon.

Michael set his heart on becoming a regular pioneer; a Jehovah's Witness who has dedicated himself on a full time basis to the work of proclaiming and teaching the good news of God's Kingdom. Prayerfully envisaging their son might one day take that step, David and Margaret Callan industriously saved regularly since his birth to make provision should he make such a munificent decision. He utilizes their providence and acquires skill in the trade of plumbing as means to support himself in the ministry.

With the forthcoming events that are prophesied to overwhelm most of mankind and rupture its flagging human ruled governments, the prescience of God's amaranthine Kingdom drew nearer its corporeal ineluctability. Contrary to popular belief, survival of the great tribulation is not contingent on hoarding money, food goods, stocks, bonds, real estate, or any other material constituent. None of which availed the multitude onboard the Titanic when it sunk, as it will also not those trusting and hoping in such, and the system that spawned them when it posthumously descends into the waters of Lethe.

The primary step towards survival is:

„Their taking in knowledge of you, the only true God, and of the one whom you sent forth, Jesus Christ. " - **John 17:3**

The Way; that leads to survival and viable only during the last days is to:

„Strip off the old personality with its practices, and clothe yourselves with the new (personality), which through accurate knowledge is being made new according to the image of the One who created it, "- **Colossians 3:9, 10**

„that you should put away the old personality which conforms to your former course of conduct and which is being corrupted according to his deceptive desires, but that you should be made new in the force actuating your mind, and should put on the new personality which was created according to God's will in true righteousness and loyalty." - **Ephesians 4:22-24**

The perennate result:
„And in response one of the elders said to me: „These who are dressed in the white robes, who are they and where did they come from?" So right away I said to him: „My lord, you are the one that knows." And he said to me: „These are the ones that come out of the great tribulation,"- **Revelation 7:14**

The greater number of mankind knew or cared little to know that survival of the great tribulation and gaining everlasting life on **earth** after Armageddon is relatively simple. It is attainable through exercising their free will and to accept the free gift from God, to seek and gain the knowledge; let it touch the heart, and thereby act upon it during the epoch of the last days. For when the inexorable Armageddon arrives, it will by then be too late.

Michael Callan is a happy young man possessing the knowledge and acting upon it even though his life is sometimes made difficult by the choice he made to be a regular pioneer. His reward though is profoundly great as he contributes in the work that is literally saving lives. His work prepares honest hearted, spiritually hungry, and humble individuals for the approaching Great Tribulation,

Armageddon, and God's Kingdom.

For those of the greater number who are ignorant of and uninterested in the Bible their lives are darkened by the critical circumstances of these last days. Stripped of all hope they cannot fathom it is due to God's chief adversary at the helm of a divinely condemned system. They nevertheless continue to put a by now vacillating wholehearted trust in the man ruled governmental system that is with celerity unraveling before them. It proves in of itself now to be the root of man's dilemma, plaguing the inhabitants of the earth whilst spiraling into ungovernable chaos.

Michael was keenly aware when he made it his aspiration to become a regular pioneer, that the enemy of God would put him to the test, placing obstacles and adversity in his path; some of which seemed insurmountable. But he thankfully makes supplication and speaks in prayer to God about his trials and asks for the strength to endure them. He now, as a young man who understands the profundity of God's word, would never pray to God to remove the impediment, but that He accords him the power of His holy spirit to endure it. His prayers were and continue to be answered. For his endurance established character, spiritual strength, and an all but impregnable shield of faith. Upon trial after trial, he gave all within his power to overcome the stumbling block, and the rest with steadfast supplication he placed in Jehovah's hands. Jehovah never left him alone or without a way to cope with the adversity, when and until it unbeknownst relinquished its grip.

Michael was twenty years of age when he met Sophia Culhane. Sophia was one year his junior. Born with the proverbial silver spoon in her mouth of parents who accrued wealth through dubious real estate and stock market investments, dearth for the material she knew not of, but all too well of it as regards the attentiveness she yearned for from her father who was consumed with acquiring affluence. Alexander Culhane was an incessant workaholic. An orphan driven by a childhood of poverty, he vowed that he would never be necessitous again.

Alexander Culhane is an atheist and holds all organized religion in contempt, especially Jehovah's Witnesses and flagrantly conveys it whenever the opportunity presents itself. He feels that their way of thinking is based on a book of myth that is as a general rule not to be taken seriously. He is unsurprisingly incensed when he discovers his daughter Sophia is studying the Bible with a Jehovah's Witness. Her mother Diane Culhane is more pragmatic and helps her husband recognize that in the world in which they live, so drastically different from their day, Sophia's association with them is better than those of her school peers, who are constantly in and out of trouble either with drugs, pre-marital sex, sexually transmitted diseases, pregnancy, or attempts at other desperate acts resulting from despondency.

Sophia became interested in the Bible through a presentation at school from a schoolmate who was born and raised as a Jehovah's Witness. That young girl knew so much about the Bible and made a very convincing case to her classmates about her beliefs and the hope she had in God's promises and His justice. Sophia longed to know more and started a Bible study with the girl which led to her growth of love of the truth of God's word, and becoming at the age of sixteen a baptized Jehovah's Witness.

At nineteen love begins to blossom between her and Michael Callan. Michael falls head over heels for her, primarily because of her love for God which she expresses w i t h such genuine simplicity of eloquence in her comments at the Christian meetings. Furthermore she is a beautiful girl with an ingenuous warm, loving nature. Her olive Italian complexion; that is her patrimony, is mellowed and tempered by the Swedish ancestry of her mother, that gives her skin a radiance that makes her the fount of envy among her schoolgirl peers. Her flaxen princess mane cascades over her shoulders, imparting the perfect frame to her cerulean eyes, perpendicular nose, high cheek bones, and her innocently inviting smile. She possesses an innate intuitiveness and can upon inquiry instantaneously see the heart of a matter. She falls in love with Michael as much as he does with her. During their courtship they are chaperoned, the custom of Christians who adhere to scriptural counsel, usually by either Sophia or Michael's mom who've grown to mutually enjoy each other's company.

Out on a date they have a late lunch and then visit the cinema and see the film „All Or Nothing"; D's debut film. As they dine Michael speaks briefly about their high school experiences on the track team together and the infraction that caused Daniel to never speak to him again. Sophia listens concernedly as he recounted the story.

„According to the news he's going to make an appearance on of all shows, the Curse God Show. ", she says in bewilderment.
„I watched ten minutes of that show before changing channels. That show hasn't a shred of dignity. He's got so much going for him I wonder why he would consent to be in any way associated with it. "
„Most people these days will do anything for money. ", Michael responds.

After the film they take a walk and exchange thoughts as they review the film. They both agree the film is an immense joy to see because of the overall cleanness of content, the myriad of emotions that leaves an indelible imprint on the heart of the viewer, an electric performance by Jason Dupree, the astounding cinematography of Old New York City, and the ending that easily cajoles a teardrop from the eye of any stoic moviegoer not easily moved to tears. It's one of the few films where people stay and read the credits if for no other reason than to read the in memory of names.
„So you enjoyed the film? ", Michael asks as they walk together.
„I did. It was great! Hard to believe they made that film without using objectionable language.
You know Michael one of the few times my father ever stopped working; he took my mom and I to New York City. I was twelve years old at the time. We saw all the sights, many of those which were in the film. ", she says sadly.
Then on a lighter note she adds,
„You know, I got a feeling while watching him dance on the staircase of that building that you'll someday see him again. That argument you had will somehow be resolved. "

They stop, gaze at each other and smile. Michael takes her left hand in both of his, holds it gently to his face, and places and affectionate kiss upon her hand. Then tenderly with the fingers of her right hand she brushes the lock of hair that swathes his brow.

He slightly inclines his head diffidently and says,

„You know I love you very much Sophia, and there is no other girl in the world I could ever imagine being with. And then he asks,

"Will you marry me Sophia? "

There's a pause; a split second of silence that seems to Michael to last an uncomfortable eternity.

Sophia looks at him with eyes that slightly betray her surprise, and then a beaming smile suddenly reflects the depth of her joy as her eyes begin to glister. She raises his head with both of her hands and their eyes meet.

„Yes, oh yes Michael", she sighs and adds smiling,

„ I love you. "

"Hold out your hand and close your eyes, darling." he requests.

Michael reaches into the inside pocket of his jacket and presents a crisp perfectly folded lace handkerchief on which the monogram SCC is embroidered, and places it in the palm of her hand.

"Open your eyes sweetheart."

She opens her eyes and says, "What a beautiful handkerchief!"

He unfolds it, and there sparkling in the dim light is a gold engagement band with two diamonds embedded in it. He takes her hand and gently slips the ring on her finger.

„Oh Michael, Michael its beautiful. ", she says as she holds her hand out before her to admire it.

As she places her head to his chest she wraps her arms around him, and let go her tears of joy. Raising her head gently with his hand under her chin he dabs the tears from her cheeks with the handkerchief and smiles; he then gives it to her. Sophia takes care of the rest. Looking him deep in the eyes, she smiles. Michael then holds her securely with his arm around her, raises her head with his fingers under her chin, and then passionately, yet with tenderness kisses her lips. The kiss leaves the both of them breathless.

They hold hands as they walk back to the car where Sophia's mom waits to drive them home; both completely enveloped in the unspoken warmth; the tingling, thrilling glow of their first kiss.

* * * *

D was having the time of his life. He's happy, as long as he's engaged in his work; he feels secure in his work, accepting unhesitatingly almost all offers to perform in the Los Angeles area. The Curse God and Live show's offer did not require him to travel, and the exorbitant fee for his services made it difficult, if not impossible to decline. Ida and Joe were vehemently opposed to D going anywhere near the „Curse God Show", but despite their protestations he did.

In intangible increments all the show business razzmatazz of this televised event served to inflate his ego. True, D has an enormous talent that set him far above his contemporaries, but the hype makes him forget almost completely the advice Joe gave him as a child; advice that as much as his talent played a significant role in his seemingly effortless rise to the top, namely his endearing humility.

During the recording of the Curse God Show D and Damon begin their close friendship. D becomes less chary around Damon and comes to unquestionably accept and believe the sycophantic adulation from the cast and crew of the Curse God show that's given him daily; a most calculated attempt on their part to conceal what lurk behind the facade. Amongst them though, an arrogant, haughty, and jokingly cynical attitude perfuse every facet of and everyone involved in the production of the show. Initially it was abhorrent to D to observe such deportment, but Damon has such an infectious way of making light fair and stark humor out of any and practically all situations, that it gradually deadened D's sense of aversion. D however for the sake of his parents made the shrewd decision to turn down the offer to act in two skits, and restricted his appearance on the show to perform his latest recording and a song together with Damon. D had worked for so many years sagaciously on his career, keeping a clear head, never indulging in the forbidden fruit that endangered as well as brought down the career and lives of many of his contemporaries in the entertainment industry. No drugs of any kind, no sexual vices, and no alcohol except for an occasional Gin Martini. He lived and loved his work.

Forbidden fruit though is the garden of Damon Marques' delight as well as many of those involved at every rung of the show.

Damon knew instinctively how to make people laugh. He had D in stitches so often that D in a bout of hysterics would beg clutching his stomach,
„Stop it Day." (His nickname for Damon)
"Damn, stop it or I'm gonna bust a gut if you don't quit".
Most times though he doesn't quit, because Damon loves to see just how crazy with laughter he can make you or an audience until you just cannot bear it any longer. Backing off only long enough to set up the next punch line and then, BAM he hit you again, and totally doubles you over.

Damon is a versatile and extremely talented comedian and rapper. He has the spontaneity and reckless nature of Richard Pryor; the agility of rhyme that Pigmeat Markham had at his command; the cutting edge cynicism of Don Rickles, and a ductile elusive play with Ebonic phrases that the principal actors of the old Amos 'n Andy television series possessed and exercised with brilliant finesse. It is not an easy undertaking for the cast of the show to work with him because he often diverts from the script and begins to ingeniously improvise, making it hard for them to stay in character with a straight face. But they respect him and learn to polish their craft while working with him.

D loved hanging out with Damon during the recording of the show. He helped him to be at ease in the ostensibly light-hearted, yet sempiternal bumptiously iniquitous atmosphere that engulfed the show like a dark dense brume. It was a time of happy reunion, reanimating their moments together on the road during their debut success of the "Kings Night" record that launched their careers. Their time together then was scanty. D was under the strict supervision of his father, and was also intermittently on tour alone with the song minus the rap for the opera coterie.

Now unencumbered by restrictive touring schedules their friendship grows deeper, well after the Curse God Show. D has a longing for those times of his high school youth, before his childhood anonymity came to an unanticipated abrupt halt; an aspect of experience he and Damon share. And Damon is exciting and fun to be with. He becomes the best friend D never had during his childhood.

They love to disguise themselves to move freely unnoticed in public. Quite often as homeless people with an appropriate exchange of attire inside of their shopping carts; appropriate to their further plans of the day. They love to travel around the streets of Los Angeles often times in a beat up looking junk-pile of a van, on its exterior, but with its interior decked with the most up to date sophisticated communications and entertainment systems.

While hanging out in the van watching the latest music videos and some of the old episodes of the Amos 'N Andy show, Damon introduces D to his first marijuana cigarette.

„Na, nah, nah, nah, nah, nah, nah! None of that simpering whimperin' half-..... inhalin'. Boy, yous gotta toke it; ta smoke it. You never get a buzz on like dat. Ya gotta toke deep ta reap. Give it heah......give it heeah. Let me sho ya. Let me sho ya how it's done. ", he says imitating Kingfish of Amos 'n Andy.

Damon's well schooled in proper British and American English, but prefers to use the language of the street and spoke Ebonics when he's being himself. Proper English is too highfallutin' for him. And he's a natural rebel especially against having to write and speak proper English which his Mom forced early upon him.

Damon snatches the thickly rolled reefer blunt out of D's hand, sits back, crosses his legs, and takes a deep drag off of the stogie. Holds it in, and exhaled with an accompanying,
„Aaaaaaaah, yeeaaaaaaaah!!! "
D's eyes bulge as he watches Damon's nose emulating a fire breathing dragon as he briskly expels two thick streams of smoke through his flared nostrils.
He hands the joint to D who does his best to do just as demonstrated. With the super singer's lungs he possesses, the inhalation went without a hitch, but is followed by a premature exhalation and a fit of coughing.
„Damn, how .....uha, uha,,,,,,,,,,,, how can you stand that stuff Damon? ", D says straining to speak.
„I likes ma reefer. It relaxes me. ", Damon replies.
„So what we gwine do tonight D? ", still speaking like Kingfish.
„What can we do? I thought I saw a REC out there before we got into the ride. I can't stand those damn cameras. I can't go anywhere without one of those things popping up. Aren't you tired of being chased by 'em?

„Hell no, I don care. I does whad I wonts to. ", says Damon as he takes another toke.

„Besides, unlikes you I likes da publicity. "

„Well I hate 'em. I wish they'd leave me alone. "

„Ya know whad I do if I didn't like 'em like you?

„No, what? "

Damon reaches under his seat and whips out a Smith and Wesson and aims it at the television screen and says,

„I'd blow 'em the .... outta de ....sky. "

D howls.

„What you doin' with a gun, Day? "

„Dis town is crazy man. You don expect me ta be roamin' deese streets heah without a piece now do ya D? Besides I love cars 'n guns. ", Damon says with the blunt hanging between his lips, eyes squinted as he gingerly strokes the pistol.

„I used a REC fo target practice once. Most times I don mind 'em, but on dis paticulah day it was buzzin' round me like a nasty ol fly. So I shot it. It made a weird whiney tech wreck kind a sound befo it fizzled out 'n died! "

„Yeah, but that's destruction of private property. Did they find out you did it? I mean it is a camera you know, and probably got a picture of you aiming at it. "

„Hell no dude, I shoot from de hip. It didn't know whad hit 'em. Ha, ha, haaaaa! I blasted dat ...... and walked away into the sunset like a ....Clint Eastwood. "

„Boy, you're crazy. ", says D.

„Hey......I got me an idea. How 'bout we go down to Twentyone tonight. Ders dis fine thang I been dying ta get next to blood, and she hangs out der wid her girls. And tonight no undercover............! We goin' down der lookin like ourselves. If any REC gets anywhere near ma boy or me I got dis laser gun Is been achin' ta try out. Dis thang wud put Darth Vader ta shame, ya hear me? "

Damon opens a drawer and takes out what looks at first to be a thick black magic marker with a wide mouth at the end and two buttons on the top of the magic marker handle. Below the wide mouth are three laser beamers and above three, all with rotating axis. He hits one button and it emits a brilliant almost blinding white light.

„Damn Day what the hell was that? "

„Ya know how dose RECS at night flash all in yo face ta get dat shot of you. Well dis thang flashes back at 'em, hones in on 'em, paralyses dey remote control function, and blasts dey ..... clear outta da........... sky. Ha, Ha, Haaaaaaah! An dey don get nuttin' in dey memory cells except fo blindin' white light."

„Where did you get that?", D asks out of combined fascination and deep curiosity.

„Ma secret fo now. Dis thang has a hundred and eighty degree radius scope and can decapilate any an all a dose .... widin dat range. You don hahdly has ta aim wid de scope on dis bad boy. Come on now D, leds go down ta Twentyone tonight. I be dyin' ta try dis thang out. Beside DJ Damnation is throwin' down tonight and he love yo music man."

„Ah, I don't know Day. This sounds too risky to me. "

„Come on D. You be playin' it safe fo fah too long. You need to shake de kinks out, befo ya too old boy. Come on now, we goin ta Twentyone and yous and me gonna have a good ol time tonight. Ain't no REC gonna bother ma boy tonight. I'll see ta dat. "

And see to it Damon did. D never had so much fun in his private life until that night. The club's patrons loved him and didn't crowd him. They were used to having stars in their midst and didn't want to risk losing their business by fawning over the stars that graced Club Twentyone. Damon finds the girl he came to Twentyone for, and with her two of her friends, one of which catches D's eye. They spend most of the time together dancing up a storm, talking, and in due course over the coming weeks D falls in love for the first time in his life with her. Unfortunately their love never stands a ghost of a chance to solidly develop because of their extreme differences in temperament and a lack of willingness on both their parts to compromise for the sake of their love.

Over the next five years D and Damon become best friends. Hanging out and laser beaming the RECS. They record some songs in D's studios one of which is released on a rap collection of Damon's. It enjoys modest success and brings them back together in concert once again, usually at D's concerts with Damon appearing as special guest.

There's a sad, melancholic side to Damon that D often can't get through to when Damon's so disposed. He would become very depressed and D knew at such times Damon was going through a three to four day alcohol and drug binge. Damon wouldn't see him or anyone for a couple of days when in such doldrums. Damon has an intrinsically keen sense of justice and often gives voice to his discontent of man's inhumanity to man, and particularly to what happened to the innocent in Old New York City. The injustices of the world thoroughly aggrieve him whenever corruption, injustice, and greed are reported. It's as if he personally, internalizes the misfortune. Damon has now recently confided in D that he's desperate to get out of his contract with the Curse God Show. Something had eruditely affected his conscience to the extent that he was in agony; an agony that stemmed from his affiliation with the show.

Despite their oft-times wild escapades, Damon knew it was important to keep D and his public image clean. It's part of his crossover appeal and mainstream success. He is proud of D's accomplishments. D was able to travel in circles that Damon didn't particularly feel comfortable in, or for that matter even want to be in the company of. And aside from being his best friend Damon is the protective older brother that D being an only child never had.

* * * *

CHAPTER THREE

THE WORLD

The greater number of the world's populace grow intolerant of religion; in particular of public expressions of Christianity. The percentage of Americans who identify with some form of Christian religion now stands at thirty-five percent according to an aggregate of Gallup Polls, a stark contrast to the year nineteen forty-eight when Gallup began tracking religious identification. The percentage at that time was ninety-one.

Reasoning it infringed on the human rights of men and women; explicitly those who favor a homosexual or lesbian way of life, the intolerance of organized religion becomes a civil rights issue. And for the sake of upholding civil rights, the word of God now constitutes harassment, an intimidation, especially to those who choose a way of life that doesn't comply with Bible standards. The homosexual agenda becomes bellicose, with constant litigations with the government, proclaiming Christian values to be bereft of "live and let live", and intrinsically wicked and evil. Moreover, Christianity as well as all other forms of organized religion impose unnecessary and unacceptable impediments on the liberty of modern life and are cited for violating the First and Fourteenth Amendments of the United States constitution as regards their objection to same sex marriage. In the most highly profiled litigation of the second decade of the twenty-first century the homosexual and lesbian movement takes their case all the way to the Supreme Court and win.

The now minority of Americans who're interested in Christianity longed to know more about the Bible's word on religion and the last days and the impending great tribulation, which now show signs of being present day society. There are now eleven and a half million Jehovah's Witnesses worldwide spreading the free gift of the knowledge of God. They're fervently working, sweeping the earth with the good news of Gods Kingdom and reaping for themselves the name; locusts, the religious pest. Doors are closing left and right in their faces, but the few who are still religiously inclined invite the Witnesses inside and speak to them about their concerns; and after having listened, really listening to those searching for truth, they offer the distressed householder a free Bible study that begins specifically with the topic of their deepest anxieties.

But just as Jesus made known by way of an illustration of the sower who sowed his seeds and the meaning of that illustration, the word of God produces the fine fruit sadly in not the majority of those dwelling on earth.

„And he again started teaching beside the sea. And a very great crowd gathered near him, so that he went aboard a boat and sat out on the sea, but all the crowd beside the sea were on the shore. [2] So he began to teach them many things with illustrations and to say to them in his teaching: [3] "Listen. Look! The sower went out to sow. [4] And as he was sowing, some [seed] fell alongside the road, and the birds came and ate it up. [5] And other [seed] fell upon the rocky place where it, of course, did not have much soil, and it immediately sprang up because of not having depth of soil. [6] But when the sun rose, it was scorched, and for not having root it withered. [7] And other [seed] fell among the thorns, and the thorns came up and choked it, and it yielded no fruit. [8] But others fell upon the fine soil, and, coming up and increasing, they began to yield fruit, and they were bearing thirtyfold, and sixty and a hundred." [9] So he added the word: "Let him that has ears to listen listen." - **Mark 4: 1-9.**

Jesus followed his illustration with its explanation:

„The sower sows the word. ¹⁵ These, then, are the ones alongside the road where the word is sown; but as soon as they have heard [it] Satan comes and takes away the word that was sown in them. ¹⁶ And likewise these are the ones sown upon the rocky places: as soon as they have heard the word, they accept it with joy. ¹⁷ Yet they have no root in themselves, but they continue for a time; then as soon as tribulation or persecution arises because of the word, they are stumbled. ¹⁸ There are still others who are sown among the thorns; these are the ones that have heard the word, ¹⁹ but the anxieties of this system of things and the deceptive power of riches and the desires for the rest of the things make inroads and choke the word, and it becomes unfruitful. ²⁰ Finally, the ones that were sown on the fine soil are those who listen to the word and favorably receive it and bear fruit thirtyfold and sixty and a hundred." - **Mark 4: 14-20**

Yet even though the word does not yield fruit with the many it does find fruition with those whose hearts are moved to action by that which they hear; bringing to fulfillment yet another Bible prophecy:

„And this good news of the kingdom will be preached in all the inhabited earth for a witness to all the nations; and then the end will come." - **Matthew 24:14**

Michael and Sophia are just two of the nearly twelve million Jehovah's Witnesses worldwide that are devoting a great number of hours dispersing the Good News of Gods Kingdom before that time arrives. Time for the world and God's chief adversary as its ruler, is apace drawing near to its grand finale.

* * * *

NEW YEAR'S DAY

D walks out the stage door onto the sidewalk into the cool San Diego night air, draws a deep breath and sighs. He stands for a moment near the backstage door and bathes in the delightfully warm feeling that's fostered by the audience's reception of the performance he just gave. Yet within him lay an underlying inexplicable sense of foreboding. Despite the initial shrug of his shoulders as if to brush it off, the feeling grows in its intensity, and it becomes apparent that there was something to it.
"What's happening?" he asks himself.
While in the limousine on his way to the hotel his thoughts play with the offer to star in a biographical film about the life of the late singer Nat King Cole. Soon his fatigue begins to forge an early morning schedule for the remainder of his stay at the Belmont Park Hotel; a long hot bath while reading the screenplay,

catch up on the televised news, and then sleep well into the first day of the New Year. While in bed with the telecom remote in his hand he slowly drifts to sleep with the sound of CNN in the background. He presses the mute button on the remote control unit of the telecom and falls into a deep slumber.

The unsympathetic incessant ring of the telephone thrusts him out of a deep tranquil comatose. He checks the time of the clock on the nightstand. It is only eight a.m. The answering device takes the call. Eavesdropping on the recorded announcement with eyes closed, he lay perfectly still waiting to catch the identity of the caller who burgled his leisure waken into the first day of the new year.

When the announcement finishes, he hears the frail voice of a woman in an almost controlled state of distress. He recognizes the voice, but in its anguish he is not able to immediately identify it for he is suddenly overwhelmed at what is conveyed in the message.

"Hello D, last night Damon took his life. They found his body this morning........." D quickly picks up the receiver now altogether propelled into cruel reality.
"Mrs. Marques what's happened?
She starts again,
"Damon took his life last night. They found his body in his car.", she begins to sob.
"Evelyn, would you like me to come by?" asks D as he wipes the sleep from his eyes.
"Would you please?"
"I'm as good as on my way." he replies.
"Listen, it won't be long before the press gets hold of this and they'll be hounding you like a dog."
At that very moment he sees on the telecom he had left on, sound muted before dozing off, the first reports and photos of Damon.
"You'd better lock all your doors and close all the blinds and curtains in the house; you know how the RECS can be. I'll see you soon." he says before he hangs up.

After calling Ben he hurriedly dresses into a pair of beige Dockers, white cotton shirt, dark blue sports jacket, and a pair of black dress sneakers. He takes the dark black sunglasses from the desk and places them in the inside breast pocket of his jacket. Cell phone beeps with the text message from Ben, "ready when you are". His cell phone notifies him of a caller. It's Aaron, D's sound engineer and close friend.
"Are you OK?" he asks.
"I just heard about Damon in the news."
"I know I just can't believe it, I haven't taken it all in yet and I'm about to go see Eve now."
"Listen D, you'll need someone with you aside from Ben to act as a buffer between you and the press. I think I should go with the both of you. I'll just hang out with Ben while you're inside with Eve, OK?
"Well alright," D replies. "When can you be ready?"

"I'm ready whenever you are."
"Good then let's go now."
"I'll be right up D."

Death's shroud of silence gird the three of them as they walk towards the service elevator to reach the hotel kitchen; and then through to the garage where their vehicle awaits them. As they make their way in and out of the corridors a vigilant taciturnity directs their steps. On continual watch they were, for the first signs of the implacable paparazzi drawn to the untimely circumstances of the loss of life; like buzzards to death's prey. Once inside of the van; the very same van that Damon eventually gave D, Ben starts the motor, and they drive off.

As they make their way towards the Los Angeles hills Ben notices a helicopter hovering above and following them.

"What did I tell you", says Ben.

„They'll go to any length to get it. They use infra-red to have a look inside of vehicles nowadays when they have a story they feel is really big and today we're the object of their affection. It's a sure bet that the RECS will be there to meet us at Eves place."

"I told her to barricade." says D.

"You can't even grieve in peace these days." adds Aaron.

Once close to the house that looks like a replica of Gracie Manor; visible is the cavalcade of media trailers and vans that have camped near the site of Evelyn Marques' residence since the story broke. Encircling the house are the RECS. The media fest in progress is immediately discernible by the sheer number of these small eyeball invaders, hovering around, over, and as it seems even under the premises of the Marques mansion, moving about at an accelerated pace, like stars in a rural night sky. These small invaders are also equipped with the most ugly of all inventions; microphones capable of eavesdropping into a rat hole while still at a great distance away from its targeted object. The targeted object was no longer just the mansion, but also the vehicle in which D Jones and his companions occupy as they approach the premises.

D rings Evelyn to inform her of their arrival at the gate. As they approach the gate it instantly swings open as if on perfect cue and just as quickly closes behind them once they've passed through. Out of the fifty or so RECS there are now at least twenty hovering around the van. Fortunately Damon had built near the garage door an entrance that functions as a kind of jet way system used at airports so that guests could enter the house undetected by the RECS. Ben pulls up to the entrance as he had done so many times before and the vehicle jet way fastens onto the entire side of the van affixing the van to the garage. Aaron places his hand on D's forearm and says,

"Ben and I are going to hang out here, but if you need us just give us the sign." In that moment D was reminded that these guys are not only his employees, but also dear friends.

Aaron opens the door and D steps out into the garage of the house. He immediately senses the encumbering grief that envelopes the house. As he walks towards the entrance of the butler's pantry, he looks to the right and sees two of Damon's most prized possessions; his automobiles. He had a thing for cars, especially German made cars. The Mercedes and his BMW are in their prospective places, but his Porsche was not there.

The house is dark and silent as he walks through the kitchen and into the living room. There sitting in a high backed chair he sees a woman's sleek arm holding a freshly lit cigarette as he approaches the room and the chair from behind.

"Eve", he calls out gently.

"It's me, D."

She rises out of the chair and turns to meet him.

Eve Marques is a petite full figured dark skinned black woman in her mid-fifties. Her hair is black with grey in just the right places. She is wearing black trousers, a black knit sweater top that has subtle sparkles of violet, green, red, and yellow therein. Her feet are bed in a pair of black house shoes. As they approach each other he sees the undeniable delineations of the not long past tears upon her face that betray the unyielding sorrow of a mother's loss of a son.

"D I'm so glad you could come. I don't know what I'd have done if you weren't here now."

"I got here as soon as I could." he says desperately fighting back the tears which threatened to weaken his resolve to be strong for her.

"Eve, what happened?"

"Have a seat." she says courteously. D sits down on the couch that made him feel as if he were alone on a life boat at sea.

"The police came by this morning." she begins.

"They told me that a man found Damon dead in his Porsche from exhaust fume asphyxiation. He had rigged a hose from the exhaust pipe that fed the fumes into the interior of the car. When they went to pull him out of the car his body slumped limp in the man's arms." she says between controlled sobs.

"It was too late. He was gone. He had written a note. The policeman gave it to me and asked me to identify his handwriting."

She goes to the bureau drawer and takes a folded letter out and hands it to D. The letter was cold as if it had been left outside all night. D unfolded it with nervous hands and begins to read:

Dear Mom,

By the time you get this letter I'll be dead. I just couldn't take it here anymore. This world is so cruel. Please do not feel sorrow for me or pity me. Be joyful knowing I've gone to a better place. Where I am now is better than anything this world could ever offer me. So please whatever you do, don't cry for me. Please don't cry for me Mom. I could never stand to see you cry and I never ever want to be the cause of pain for you. You are better off without me unhappy here. That is all I want to say before I go. I couldn't have asked for a better Mom than you, but I have to go now. Tell D he's the only true friend I ever had and that I hope he has at least one more song left for me.

All my Love,

Damon

A lump swells in D's throat as he reads the last sentence and the tears begin to flood his eyes to the point that he can't focus on the writing in Damon's letter any longer. But he wants to see the writing. He needs to see what Damon's written. So he struggles over and over again to read that last sentence, over and over again, and then back to the top as if committing the letter to memory. He then places the letter on the coffee table and pulls the handkerchief from out of the inside pocket of his sports jacket and holds it to his eyes. He dabs his eyes with it, in an attempt to prevent the tears from making an appearance. But they are undeniably the first of many tears that he would shed. For his best friend Damon was now gone.

* * * *

It's strange, mysterious, and even ironic how life deals you a blow, but at the same time gives you the strength along with the circumstances to endure it. D needed time away from the stage to handle the death of his best friend and fortunately enough his next concert was a Valentine's Day engagement. The question that crosses his mind over and over again is, „Why Damon? Why didn't you call? “. D feels responsible for his friend's death, for being so busy that he didn't try harder to reach Damon. He had tried though, but Damon had his answering machine on as a buffer between him and the world, and wasn't letting anyone in. That served only to frustrate and sometimes anger D. The last time they saw each other Damon told him that he wanted out of the Curse God Show and said that he felt the show was a, "What was the word he used?" D thought to himself. An abomination, y e s , an abomination was the word he used. He expressed to D that he felt his talent was being abused. He hated the show and all it stood for.

Two weeks after the funeral Eve calls D to let him know that there are a few things of Damon's that she wants him to have and one item that was found in the Porsche with him on that tragic night, that Damon especially wanted him to have. While visiting her she gives him the watch that Damon was particularly fond of, and a Bible.

As she hands him the book she says,

„This was found near him in the car. He had written something to you on the inside of it. “, she adds smiling with a quiet sense of pride.

D opens the book and to the left on the inside he reads,

„Hey Blood, I want you to have this book, but above all else I want you to read it. Please D, read it and don't be afraid. It can be heavy at times, so I advise you to start with the book of Psalms and Proverbs. You'll know where to go from there. Your Friend, Day. “

Feeling as if he had been hit by a ton of bricks, D slumps down onto the sofa and sits. Damon never wrote in Ebonics, but having read the final words from Damon to him, it was like hearing Damon's voice speaking to him the way he loved to express himself most.

„Nothing brings me more joy out of this entire tragic ordeal than knowing that

Damon started reading the Bible before.........."; E v e couldn't bring herself to finish the sentence.

D didn't stay long with Eve. It was difficult for the both of them right now. A short visit was the most that Eve or D could presently bear.

* * * *

Once home he gets comfortable and goes back to bed. He doesn't feel like doing much of anything these days, not even eating. He lay there for a few minutes and then gets up and takes the Bible that Eve had given him out of his backpack and then goes back to bed. He raises the back of the bed with the remote control to his favored position for reading and turns on his reading light. He closes the light tight curtains over all the bedroom windows because he doesn't want to know what time of day it is. So his bedroom is flooded in total darkness except for the lamp.

He opens the book and reads Damon's words again and cries. When the wave of sorrow subsides he opens to the book of Proverbs and begins to read:

„1 The proverbs of Sol′o·mon the son of David, the king of Israel, ² for one to know wisdom and discipline, to discern the sayings of understanding, ³ to receive the discipline that gives insight, righteousness and judgment and uprightness, ⁴ to give to the inexperienced ones shrewdness, to a young man knowledge and thinking ability.
⁵ A wise person will listen and take in more instruction, and a man of understanding is the one who acquires skillful direction, ⁶ to understand a proverb and a puzzling saying, the words of wise persons and their riddles.
⁷ The fear of Jehovah is the beginning of knowledge. Wisdom and discipline are what mere fools have despised.............

2 My son, if you will receive my sayings and treasure up my own commandments with yourself, ² so as to pay attention to wisdom with your ear, that you may incline your heart to discernment; ³ if, moreover, you call out for understanding itself and you give forth your voice for discernment itself, ⁴ if you keep seeking for it as for silver, and as for hid treasures you keep searching for it, ⁵ in that case you will understand the fear of Jehovah, and you will find the very knowledge of God." ⁶ For Jehovah himself gives wisdom; out of his mouth there are knowledge and discernment. ⁷ And for the upright ones he will treasure up practical wisdom; for those walking in integrity he is a shield, ⁸ by observing the paths of judgment, and he will guard the very way of his loyal ones. ⁹ In that case you will understand righteousness and judgment and uprightness, the entire course of what is good.

D pauses, and thinks about what he's just read, and then read chapter two verses one through nine again. And then suddenly, resurgent waves of comforting stillness, and peace, enfold him completely upon ruminating on the words recorded by King Solomon. He then switches out the light and falls into a deep sleep. He awakens ten hours later. The first rest he's had since the beginning of the New Year; and Damon's funeral.

Upon awakening he makes his way to the kitchen. His cook had prepared for him a meal; chicken salad, a fresh mixed salad, mashed potatoes, and brown gravy. D microwaves the potatoes and gravy and made himself a chicken salad sandwich and eats. Having satiated his physical hunger he goes back to bed and begins reading more from the book of Proverbs.

Over the next weeks he consumes more and more of the Bible's spiritual fare, and after having finished the books of Psalms and Proverbs he then starts with the Gospels. Upon completing the books of Matthew, Mark, Luke, and John he asks himself, „Why aren't these teachings mandatory in school? ". Peace would reign throughout the earth if the laws that Jesus spoke of were mandatory and practiced by all. Then quite suddenly, one thing became absolutely crystal clear to him: Any religion that professed to be true and congruous to the Bible's scriptures wo u l d vehemently object and stand in opposition to any of their member's participation in war of any kind. Of this he was completely convinced.

* * * *

„Accordingly I say to YOU, Keep on asking, and it will be given YOU; keep on seeking, and YOU will find; keep on knocking, and it will be opened to YOU."   -LUKE 11:9

It's now April and D is performing in concert in San Luis Obispo, California. After the last encore he returns to his dressing room and there on the table are a dozen long-stemmed white roses with a card and also a book next to the vase. The delicate scent of the flowers accentuates and underscores the atmosphere of the room. He opens the envelope and reads the card:

Dear Daniel,
    Your performance was sensational tonight. We enjoyed your show immensely. Hope you like roses. If not maybe there is someone you'd like to pass them on to. Hope however you will take the time to read the book.
Yours,
Sophia and Michael Callan

„It can't be. Not Mike Callan from the high school track team." He takes a closer look at the small book that lay at the foot of the vase. „What YOU Need to Know About What the Bible Really Teaches" is the title. It is Mike Callan, well whad do ya know! He wonders if he's still there among the fans that usually wait around to see him back stage after the concerts. He races to the door and tells security to let them through if they're among the crowd. He then grabs a towel, wipes the sweat from his brow, and checks his appearance in the mirror, and then the knock on the door.

He opens the door and there in front of him is an incredibly beautiful young woman and a mature Mike Callan.

„I don't believe it. I just don't believe it! What are you doing here? ", D says before they embrace like old friends.

„We came to see your show and thought we might be able to see you. Daniel, I mean D this is my wife Sophia. "

D and Sophia's eyes meet.

„Hello, it's a pleasure to meet you D. "

„The pleasure is all mine Sophia. Jeez Mike you really know how to pick 'em. Please come in. "

They enter the well lit and understated modern decor of the dressing room suite.

„You really do get the star treatment, huh? " says Michael as he looks around the room.

D shrugged and says,

„They treat me alright, most times. At other times it might surprise you what one must stipulate in a contract in order to get it.

Would you like something to drink? There's plenty here at the bar. "

„What would you like dear, Mineral Water with lemon? ", Michael asks.

Sophia affirmatively nods in accord.

D plays bartender and pours all three of them a glass of mineral water, then adds fresh lemon slices and invites them to have a seat around the bar.

„Tell me Mike, did you pursue track and field after graduation? "

„No, after what happened in New York City my life took a much different course. " D's face drops in sadness.

„Yeah, that left a lasting mark on most of our lives. ", D replies.

„I'm sorry D, I didn't mean to bring back painful memories. "

„No, it's alright. I was more fortunate than most having survived." D then suddenly changes his somber tone.

"Hey, thanks for the roses. They really brighten up the room. When I read the card I wasn't sure if it was you or some other person with the same name. It sure is good to see you. So what have you been doing? "

„Well like you I'm doing what I've been doing since we were kids. Spreading the good news of Gods Kingdom and teaching people and helping them become acquainted with the Bible; the both of us. ", Michael glances and nods to Sophia.

A look of puzzlement comes over D's face.

„You get paid to do that. "

Michael and Sophia look at each other and chuckle.

„In a sense yes, but no, not with a paycheck or anything like that. It may be hard to believe but when a person simplifies his life he realizes that it takes very little to live comfortably. And believe it or not God provides. "

„You know Michael, for the first time in my life a few months ago I started reading the Bible. There's so much truth in it, but I'm afraid there's a lot of it that baffles me."

„What made you interested in reading the Bible D? ", asks Sophia.

„A very good friend gave me a Bible before he died? In my sorrow I started reading the books from the Bible he suggested I read. Surprisingly it gave me a great deal of comfort. But there's something I just don't understand and that is the whole idea of the resurrection. The Bible speaks about the earth being restored and the meek inheriting the earth. It is also written that those ruining the earth will come to ruin. I always believed when you die you either go to heaven or hell, but lately I've read passages that lead me to believe that the earth will continue to exist with righteous people, good people only living on it. I don't know. "

Michael and Sophia hang on every word that D speaks. When he had finished there was a somewhat uncomfortable pause for D before Michael finally says, „That is very sound reasoning D. You HAVE been reading the Bible and you ask questions that most people never even think of asking even after having read the Bible for years. You probably haven't had time, but have you had a look at the book we sent with the roses? "

„No, just long enough to realize that it was you who were calling. Then I asked security to see if you were still there. "

D walks over to the table where the book lay. He picks it up and reads the title aloud.

„What YOU Need to Know About What the Bible Really Teaches. "

„I think if you take a closer look, you will get reliable answers with scriptural support to the questions you have. ", says Michael.

The sound of the crowd outside grew louder with some of them chanting, „We want D. We want D. "

All three of them look for a moment in the direction of the door.

„ D, I know you have a lot of fans out there who would love to see you and we don't want to take up too much of your time,", Sophia says.

„but if you'd like we'd love to have you over for a meal. It would be a great way for you and Michael to talk and................

„I'd love to. " D interjects.

„How can I contact you? "

„Michael's card is inside of the book. ", she replies.

D opens the book and finds the card.

„Can I call you tomorrow? " D asks.

Sophia and Michael stay with D a few minutes more, before leaving out of consideration for the eager fans who were waiting outside. Out of all of the fans that visit who knew him from high school, never before has he ever had the feeling that there was one that could help him in his search for answers, as he felt with Michael and Sophia's visit. He was with anticipation looking very much forward to seeing them again soon.

* * * *

„and YOU will know the truth, and the truth will set YOU free." -JOHN 8: 32

How often does it occur that when a dear friend departs, a door opens that suddenly makes way for another to enter? Such was the case with D, Damon, and Michael. D didn't waste time. He called Michael the very next day and had lunch with Michael and Sophia at their home two days later. They reminisced over the high school days on the track team and the sucker punch. Michael was finally able to give in full the apology D the day after the incident interrupted and would not accept. An adult D now accepts, and apologizes to Michael for having spoken the barbed words that sparked their adolescent brawl.

Over the next three years D found not only in Michael a staid bridge to his childhood, but also an able teacher to assist him in understanding the profundities of the Bible. He studied the Bible with Michael on a bi-weekly basis. He had difficulty at first with the explication on much spiritual subject matter until clear scriptural evidence was given him to substantiate that it was without a shadow of a doubt, God's view on the disputed issue. Through his studies he learned from the scriptures that man has and continues to adulterate Gods word and stance to suit his pleasures; but by means of a conscientious examination of the scriptures, the light of its truth shines like a beacon in the stygian darkness of God's chief adversary's world. And it's truth yields a plenteous healing that slowly but thoroughly extirpates the fatal sting of Satan's deliberately misleading doctrinal fallacies; either causing one to compliantly espouse its corrective counsel, or contumaciously abandon God's Word completely.

D would debate considerably with Michael, yet D had become a young man of reason, capable of sagacious illation. He loves to research and after having done so discovers the path to "the way" that Michael directs and instructs him is scripturally veracious. His first visit to the Kingdom Hall left him at first bemused. No crucifixes, images, or grand choirs singing hyperbolized Hallelujahs. Instead all raised their voices in praise to Jehovah God with Kingdom Songs three times during the course of the meeting. There was a thirty minute discourse by the speaker always with references throughout his discourse to the scriptures, and an hour Watchtower study where all participated in giving answers to the roughly seventeen questions outlined in the study. He left each meeting with a more in depth comprehensive understanding of the scriptures, a strengthening of his faith, and his knowledge and love for God.

In the world's efforts to find the perpetrators of the nuclear attack on New York City the U.S. government and the FBI were allegedly inefficacious. With the U.N. and its military force NATO now at the helm of world security, the FBI and the commander and chief of the United States of America could no longer exercise carte blanche to declare war without impermeable evidence to support its justification. So a scheme is embarked on by the Global Elite to inculpate religious groups of allegedly seeking to wage war with terror in the name of ordained justice. And because religion is the undeviating target of hostility of the twenty-first century's civil rights movement, it is categorically decided that the enemy to attack and devour is organized religion. After all there's so much sexual abuse and injury to youth committed by false religion, in particular with the clergy of the Catholic Church, that makes it an effortless maneuver to muster support to completely burn her up in the fire of their rage. An all out campaign begins against the practice of organized religion and assemblage of any and all religious groups amongst themselves; depicted by the media as the saboteurs of civil rights, the institutions of sexually deviant miscreants, and the effigy of nuclear terrorism.

Unbeknownst to the American people capitalism had spawned irremediable widespread corruption in the political realm and had reached its pinnacle during the conclusion of the last days; the likes of which would make Richard M. Nixon's and George W. Bush's presidential incumbencies appear saintly and irreproachable by comparison. By manipulating the U.N. and the world leaders, the Global Elite now unscrupulously scheme to obliterate religion globally, by pointing an incriminating finger aimed directly at the contemporary putative enemy of world peace and security; Organized Religion. Cogently staged video images begin to appear on the internet and televised news channels of churches used specifically as the operational location to plot the nuclear attack on New York City. Especially targeted are Christian churches where the greater numbers of its members are foreigners. Churches and Congregations where people from all nations come together without prejudice amongst themselves to worship and get to know the true God through intense study of His word found in the Bible, are first and foremost accused as the perpetrators of wickedness and evil. These people are depicted as the spearheads of terrorism. The intent of these bedfellow political leaders, civil rights groups, and capitalist monopolies is to sway public opinion in accord with their agenda; that organized religion required obligatory abolition. In THIS endeavor they succeed!

The grand finale is devised to give additional clout to their odious allegations and to cinch the success of their nefarious campaign. A small but effective dirty biological and nuclear bomb is planted and explodes in Hyde Park, Central London, England, annihilating and critically injuring thousands and effectually making Central London and the surrounding area a wasteland for some years to come. And as with the attacks that razed the World Trade Center Towers, the alleged „suicide" death of Marilyn Monroe, and many other major events that mark time in the lives of countless generations; the absolute truth concerning these events would not be disclosed until after Armageddon. In the short-term memory of the American general public, the New York City nuclear attack, like September 11, 2001 quickly evanesces in the plumbless filament of the world's incoherent secular history. But this newly staged attack on Great Britain would elicit the public's sense of urgency and outrage, to ensure the forthcoming success of their diabolical plot.

Panic spreads like wildfire anew throughout the world. This time around the (now "outed" as the ritualistic Satan worshipers they've always been) multi-trillionaire Global Elite, orchestrate more misleading film footage of a religious group's secret cabal on London. Great Britain and the American governments are now able to inveigle the United Nations and NATO to establish and enforce laws world-wide banning organizational religion. The government is able to induce the public to go along with its agenda through fear, effectively fostered through mainstream media. Within weeks these laws are implemented and imposed on all organized religions. From Catholics to Protestants, Buddhists, Muslims, all the way down to the smallest groups; are now bound by law to cease organized public assemblage and public interpretation of their doctrines and/or teaching of the Holy Scriptures. Millions of churches world-wide are shutdown and their assets including real estate are confiscated. This has a twofold purpose of allegedly „restoring world peace", and the yield of revenue and real estate for the bankrupt government coffers. The icons and relics of these churches that do not render inalienable revenue are burned completely in balefires and smelted for their precious metals.

Global governments, in particular the American government, has bailed out so many private corrupt capitalist institutions, banks, and industries over the past two decades that it tapped-out with a subsequent collapse and complete fall of the Dollar and is in desperate need of a brobdingnagian pecuniary infusion. With the overthrow and fall of organized religion they now reap a voluminous spoil. The manhunt is now on. A rigorous application of the law is imposed: The right to buy or sell is refused any group or individual, if any affiliation to organized religion by the government is discovered or suspected. All those who do business with organized religion are now mourning the loss of her at a distance. The travelling merchants, ship captains, and all who make a living and became rich through her, mourn at a distance. At a distance, out of fear of the confiscation of THEIR assets, if THEY were to draw too near to her in bereavement.

* * * *

THE LAST DAYS AND THE GREAT TRIBULATION GOD'S CHIEF ADVERSARY'S INDICTMENT OF MANKIND

„Happy is he who reads aloud and those who hear the words of this prophecy, and who observe the things written in it, for the appointed time is near." - Revelation 1:3

How could anyone be happy reading the book of Revelation? A Bible book that is far too complicated to understand and full of expressions that conjure in the mind of the reader horrific terrifying visions. Perhaps it brings happiness to face fear and thereby undo it. Henry David Thoreau wrote, „Nothing is so much to be feared as fear. " By daring to read the Revelation of Christ in the apostle John's book of Revelation, you will completely dismantle the fear which arises from the unfamiliar and unexplored. The fear will then be superseded by reverential awe and great joy when its „frightful" visions are once and for all time accurately revealed and the subsequent good news for mankind's survival is clarified.

In the book of Revelation, we find described the last days of Satan and his end. Revelation discloses that at the time of Christ's taking kingdom power, Satan is hurled down out of heaven to the earth, no longer having access to the heavens, as he did in the days of Job and for centuries thereafter: **Revelation 12:7-12**. After this defeat Satan has only a „short period of time", during which he makes war with „the remaining ones of (the woman's) seed, who observe the commandments of God and have the work of bearing witness to Jesus". In his efforts to devour the remaining ones of the woman's seed, he is called „the dragon, "a swallower or crusher. In the earlier description of his fight against the woman and his efforts to devour her man child, he is pictured as „a great fiery-colored dragon. " **Revelation 12:3, 4**.

The book of Job poignantly draws back the curtain of the heavens, for a glimpse into the events there and on earth during Job's day before God's chief adversary was hurled to the earth. The introductory narrative of the book of Job describes a gathering in heaven where the angels took their station before God. Satan was also present, and he leveled charges against Job. Job was a „man proved to be blameless and upright, and fearing God and turning aside from bad." The Devil had claimed that Job, and outstanding servant of God, would not remain loyal if he lost his material possessions. Job was a man who possessed great wealth. Why did not God, Sovereign of all creation, ignore Satan's accusations or destroy him? He knew that would not effectively resolve the issue that had been raised, and hence allowed Job to be tested through tribulation by Satan.

The book of Job identifies Satan as mankind's merciless enemy. Between the gathering in heaven at **Job 1:6** and the one described at **Job 2:1** an unspecified period of time passed, during which Job was cruelly put to the test, Jobs loyalty however withstood that test. But Satan did not admit that his claims had been proved wrong. On the contrary, he demanded that Job be put to another severe test. Thus, the Devil tested Job both when he was prosperous and when he was destitute, demonstrating beyond a shadow of a doubt, that God's chief adversary has no compassion for the needy or for victims of calamity.

Then Satan further claimed that ANY human would turn away from God, abandoning their integrity if they suffered physically.
„Skin in behalf of skin, and everything that a MAN has he will give in behalf of his soul. For a change, thrust out your hand, please and touch as far as his bone and his flesh (and see) whether he will not curse you to your very face", said Satan. - **Job 2: 4, 5**
„„Accordingly God said to Satan:
„There he is in your hand! Only watch out for his soul itself! "
So Satan went out away from the person of God and struck Job with a malignant boil from the sole of his foot to the crown of his head. And he proceeded to take for himself a fragment of earthenware with which to scrape himself and he was sitting in among the ashes. Finally his wife said to him:
„Are you yet holding fast your integrity? Curse God and die!"
But he said to her:

„As one of the senseless women speaks, you speak also. Shall we accept merely what is good from the (true) God and not accept also what is bad? In all this Job did not sin with his lips.““

Unaware of Satan's role in all of this, Job could not understand why God allowed him to experience these trials. Still Job never turned against God. Job suffered and endured tribulation, yet his integrity was not forsaken. Job's faithfulness proved once again that God's chief adversary is a relentless liar. After his tribulation Jehovah God, being „very tender in affection and merciful, “ restored Job's health, gave him double his previous wealth, and blessed him with ten children. - **James 5:11, Job 42:10** By keeping integrity to God while under severe trial, Job successfully answered Satan's indictment that all humans will not remain faithful to God if put to the test.

The story of Job is one of many about the faith and endurance of those under tribulation. As recorded by the Apostle Paul in the book of **Hebrews chapter eleven** he alludes to the many faithful and adds in verse thirty-two „And what more shall I say? For the time will fail me if I go on to relate about Gideon, Barak, Samson, Jephthah, David as well as Samuel and the (other) prophets who through faith defeated kingdoms in conflict, effected righteousness, obtained promises, stopped the mouths of lions, stayed the force of fire, escaped the edge of the sword, from a weak state were made powerful..........“.

God's chief adversary could care less about those who don't know or haven't found „the true God“. With them he has already accomplished his chief purpose and goal. They are, and unless they actively seek the true God, remain in darkness thoroughly misled and misleading others to „destination destruction“, along with God's chief adversary, and his world. For even now, as back then with Adam and Eve; in this system (world) that we are currently living, Satan ALWAYS has a catch 22 affixed to all of his enticements. None of us who dwell on the earth escapes this inevitable fact of Satan's system when we run after the world's purported „you need this on your get list" in order to attain happiness. It is his way of keeping the world's attention away from him and his purpose, but more importantly though to keep mankind in the dark as to God's true purpose for mankind.

Once you have found God and set your life in harmony with living according to His higher standards rather than those of Satan's world, sincerely from the heart to the best of your ability, you can unequivocally then expect to face extreme opposition, temptation, and/or tribulation. Whether it be from family, friends, associates, employers, or co-workers; the pressure will be put upon you to ease up or drop completely your adherence and obedience to God's laws found in the Bible. By endeavoring to bring your life in harmony with Bible standards you will have then joined the ranks of those who are direct targets of Satan, whose integrity MUST be broken. He will pull out of his bag of tricks, every trick in his book to exploit your weaknesses. This is what he does best! Do not be discouraged though because the happiness and reward of this course of living is unimaginably great indeed. For you are not alone:

„No temptation has taken you except what is common to men. But God is faithful, and he will not let you be tempted beyond what you can bear, but along with the temptation he will also make the way out in order for you to be able to endure it. " - **First Corinthians 10:13**.

In the course of your faithfulness to God, Satan will come and go with persistence, with test after test attempting to break your integrity and the close relationship you have now established with God. If you don't belief what is written to be true, then live by the laws of the Bible without compromise to the very best of your ability, and then observe closely the opposition, temptation, and/or tribulation that begins to present itself in your life. Obedience to God's laws in and of itself establishes a strong foundation for an intimate personal relationship with Him. Remain obedient and He will deliver you through any tribulation which His adversary puts upon you.

The tests that the faithful presently endure are only minute rehearsals for the forthcoming great tribulation where each and every individual on earth at that time must personally decide on which side of the fence they will stand or fall. There will come a time as in the days of Noah when God closed the door of the ark, and even the good people of Noah's day perished because they did not listen to Noah as he prepared himself and those who listened for survival. Jehovah God will also close the door to salvation from the ungodly world of His chief adversary.

These are the last days of Satan's world. Those who have made the decision to be faithful to God, and have accumulated experience and a track record of faithfulness will find it easier to say „No" once again to God's infamous chief adversary; especially when he puts the thumb screws on ALL those dwelling on earth. He will apply merciless pressure through his human agents who outnumber the human faithful; and with his spirit agents (angels turned demons) who fortunately for the human faithful, are outnumbered by Jehovah God's angelic forces. Consequently, as in the days of the prophet Elisha, the faithful steadfast integrity keepers know that during the great tribulation that will usher in Armageddon; they can, and confidently will say as Elisha and Azariah did, „Do not be afraid, nor be terrified........ on account of all the crowd that is with him, for there are more who are with us than those who are with them. "- **2 Kings 6:16, 2 Chronicles 32:7, 2 Thessalonians 1: 6-10**

* * * *

"We must obey God as ruler rather than men. " - ACTS 5:29

The eradication of all organized religion is swift in its execution but by no means thoroughly complete. Purportedly, it's of no consequence to the recently established One World United Global Government whether any particular religion is casuistry or the unadulterated truth. Where civil rights laws against discrimination based on race, color, religion, national origin, or disability are preserved; worldwide across the board those laws as regards religion are countermanded. The line of delineation has been drawn. On the face of it, between global peace and security, versus religious permissiveness; au fond between God and Satan. It is a delineating line that separates the faithful from the unfaithful, dividing households from within, separating those who obey men as rulers from those who obey God as ruler.

„He said to them: „Isaiah aptly prophesied about you hypocrites, as it is written, „This people honor me with (their) lips, but their hearts are far removed from me. It is in vain that they keep worshiping me, because they teach as doctrines commands of men. Letting go the commandment of God, you hold fast the tradition of men. ", - **Mark 7:6-8**

With the world's events unfolding as they are; the trustworthy light of God's word becomes conclusively brighter and its wisdom more comprehendible now in its near complete fulfillment. This wisdom however is not from or of the world's celebrated scholars; it is divine wisdom found only in God's word the Bible, and is completely lost on the rest of the world who actively or inactively choose to uphold the laws that now ostracize God's faithful.

"At that time Jesus said in response: "I publicly praise you, Father, Lord of heaven and earth, because you have hidden these things from the wise and intellectual ones and have revealed them to babes." - **Matthew 11:25**

With the divisive doctrines of false religion now completely exposed and dismantled, a small minority of TRULY FAITHFUL Christians who escaped the grasps of false religion, now ally themselves to those who have sounded the warning horn door to door to their neighbors for over a century, and recognize the gravity of the fundamental principle of holding fast their integrity and allegiance to God. The ever increasing brightness of the incontrovertible accurate knowledge of God is what spawns an alliance that eventually binds them in love for God and one another.

Initially assemblage for the purpose of religious worship to God was punishable by fines or imprisonment of up to one year or both. Stiffer penalties followed on the heel of chronic abuse of the law. The Faithful understand though that assemblage for the purpose of brotherly encouragement, is not an option, but a requirement by God for anyone wishing to love, trust, and serve Him wholeheartedly. Jehovah's Witnesses are the largest of all the outlawed religious groups who still strictly adhere to the scriptural directives found in the book of **Romans chapter one verses eleven and twelve:**

„For I am longing to see you, that I may impart some spiritual gift to you in order for you to be made firm; or, rather, that there may be an interchange of encouragement among you, by each one through the other's faith, both yours and mine."

and in the book of **Hebrews chapter ten verses twenty-four and twenty-five**:

„And let us consider one another to incite to love and fine works, not forsaking the gathering of ourselves together, as some have the custom, but encouraging one another, and all the more so as you behold the day drawing near."

And all the more so as you behold the day drawing near.

The governing body of the Jehovah's Witnesses boldly herald in the Watchtower magazine,
„The Great Tribulation Is Here!"
So begin the secret meetings of God's faithful worshipers who loyally congregate in His name throughout the world.

Due to their vigilant watch on the world's state of affairs, property and asset confiscation is minimal within the organization of Jehovah's Witnesses. They stress in their published literature the biblical import of simplifying one's life from any unnecessary abundance of material possessions, and practiced what they published. The difference between Jehovah's Witnesses and the rest of the religions of the world is that they are more than just acquainted with the Bible. They read it daily and understand it well enough to fearlessly descry, the foretoken curve ball that now confounds the rest of the world alienated from the ACCURATE knowledge of God. The Witnesses and the rest of a smaller group of faithful are exuberant, having discerned that with the inception of the Great Tribulation, the cleansing of the earth and the destruction of all its wicked elements is very, very near. For they know that the ambit of the Great Tribulation will reach its palpable prophetic fulfillment at the inevitable battle of Armageddon; a battle in which they perform no physical combat whatsoever. They need only stand still with confidence and see Jehovah, his mighty son Jesus, and His myriad of angels; charge ahead in battle, for His names' sake, and on their behalf.
- Second Chronicles 20:17

D bought a home in Bradley, California six months after Michael and Sophia visited him backstage in order to study on a regular basis with Michael in Parkfield, California. D was baptized two years after he began to study with Michael, yet was totally taken aback by the pernicity the interdict on organized religion came to fulfill the Bible prophecy of Babylon the Great, just one year later. It is one thing to learn about Bible prophesy, yet another to actually see it strike the world in such a rapaciously recondite manner, and with lightning rapidity. When he finished his concert tour he decides to take a break from work and learn as much as he could about God's word, especially in light of it's now distinct and undeniable correlation to the state of affairs of the world. The mainstream media gives an abundance of the world's view of affairs, easily accessible by watching the news on television, the internet, or from the few news papers still in existence. Mainstream media is now firmly in the grip of the Order of Satanic Worshippers (the Global Elite and their henchmen), whose primary objective is to bruit disinformation and continue to dominate and mislead the world through their One World United Global Government.

Michael is an elder at their congregation and is very active in arranging logistics for the secret meetings of the congregation. He's been arrested more than once and has a reputation with the law. Those at the FBI want him "put out of the way". Michael for his part continues to do his work in earnest knowing that there is nothing they or anyone for that matter, can do to bring an end to the pure worship of God on earth. Never has man in biblical, as well as secular history been able to annihilate the pure worship of Jehovah God on earth. D however is concerned for Michael because he's rubbed shoulders with many of those politicians and world leaders while active in the entertainment industry. He often hears how they detest Jehovah's Witnesses and feel the best thing to do is to rid the world of the whole lot. D supports the congregation and Michael, giving his time and financial support to help the faithful worldwide, in every way that he can.

While having dinner with Michael and Sophia he tries his best to convince Michael to lay extra low for a while.

„I'm afraid for you Michael." D says in a somber tone.

Sophia's eyes quickly glance demurely past D's in silent approval as she pours D a glass of red wine.

„I've been preparing for a job for the opera buffs in Los Angeles and have been getting some strange inquiries about my affiliation with you. I thought to myself why are they asking me questions about you? Then I thought, it's no secret, the world knows that I became a Jehovah's Witness. And now that you've become somewhat of a Jesse James figure in your own right, I get the feeling they're just waiting to catch you in organizing another of our meetings and then lower the boom on you."

„Maybe you shouldn't do that job in Los Angeles D." replies Michael while polishing off the last of his first helping of spaghetti.

„I have to. I'm the guest of honor. It may even incur suspicions if I don't attend." says D.

„You've got a point there. But on the other hand these are extremely perilous times we're in now." Michael says and then pauses in silent contemplation.

„Look, I promise to be a bit more cautious with the work if it'll ease my brothers mind." Michael adds smiling.

„Besides, Fia (Michael's pet name for Sophia) has been on me, concerned about my safety and that I should share more of the responsibilities with the others in the congregation instead of trying to be a one man band."

Sophia walks from the kitchen to where Michael is seated, runs her hand through his hair, and kisses him on the forehead, then takes his empty plate and places another portion of spaghetti on the table for him.

„Honey, we just want to keep you away from any unnecessary harm." she says before going back to the kitchen.

„I want you to do me a favor." says D.

He hands Michael a beeper device and a set of keys.

„With all these questions that have been coming my way about you I'd feel better if you'd carry this with you at all times, especially now with this gig I have in L.A. If these questions continue while I'm down there and the situation becomes......

D pauses to search for the word, well....., HOT, I want you to have this and use it if necessary. If this beeper goes off then you'll know it is a signal from me for you to flee. Get out of Dodge. The keys are to a cottage I have in Lake Tahoe. I own the property, but the title is listed under the name of Joe Meager. Don't ask me how I did it. I just did it, OK! You and Sophia will be safe there for awhile."

„Geez, now you're starting to make me nervous D. What's going on? "

„I don't know exactly." says D in a slightly raised tone of voice.

„It just gave me the creeps the way your name kept coming up while working on the preparations for this show at the Ahmanson."

The both of them stop and ponder the situation silently then D walks over to where Michael is sitting and places his hand on his shoulder and says,

„We've been given constant reminders lately from the governing body to take special heed to the words at Matthew ten sixteen, have we not? "

Michael then quoted the scripture aloud having committed it to memory.

"Look! I am sending YOU forth as sheep amidst wolves; therefore prove yourselves cautious as serpents and yet innocent as doves."

Michael then puts his left hand over D's hand resting on his shoulder and replies,

„The student now sharpens the teacher's pencil. You've learned well."

„I'll see you when I'm back from L.A., O.K.? Sophia that was a grand super as always."

Sophia appears in the kitchen doorway.

„Aren't you staying for dessert? "

D turns to Sophia and says,

„Thanks, will take a rain check, I've got a few things to prepare before leaving."

While heading out the door D thought to himself, "Sophia's put on a few pounds."

* * * *

„for then there will be great tribulation such as has not occurred since the world's beginning until now, no, nor will occur again." -MATTHEW 24:21

„Five minutes Mr. Jones. ", calls the voice from the other side of D's dressing room door at the Ahmanson theatre.

With the five minute stage call D's journey into the past, along with his Martini, ends, as he returns to the reality of the evenings events that are about to begin.

He takes one last look in the floor to ceiling mirror and heads for the door.

Suddenly another knock on his door and a voice asks,

„D Jones?"

„Yes. " D answers.

„Open the door, we're from the Federal Bureau of Investigation. "

As if by reflex D bolts quietly to his open backpack and finds the beeper and hits the button three times, then throws the beeper back in his bag.

He then says,

„Just a moment please. ", and then goes to the door.

He opens the door and on the other side are two men dressed in black suits, with white shirts and ties. They hold up their badges and formally introduce themselves,

„I'm special agent Gallager and my associate agent Morton. We'd like to ask you some questions about a Mr. Michael Callan. "

„Yes, I would like to accommodate you, but I'm due to go onstage soon. "

The two agents enter the room menacingly as D steps back.

„That can wait. We've informed the director of the show that you'll be delayed. How long have you known Michael Callan? "

„Since high school. "

„Are you aware that he's been organizing secret religious meetings? "

„Am I allowed to call my lawyer before you proceed any further along this line of questioning? "

„Mr. Jones we know that you are a Jehovah's Witness who has attended secret meetings. Now you have the choice of either answering our questions here without your lawyer or down at the station with him. What'll it be? "

„I'd like to call my lawyer. "

„Have it your way Mr. Jones. "

      D goes to the phone on the dressing room table and makes the call and explains the situation. His lawyer asks D to put the investigators on the phone, but they refuse to oblige and told D to tell him that they are taking him into custody for knowledge of the whereabouts of a public offender of the law. They tell D where they are taking him and that he's free to pass that information to his lawyer. D then gives his lawyer the information, tells his lawyer to meet him there, hangs up, and that is when they handcuff him and read him his rights.

„I don't believe this! You have no right to do this. ", D says in a fearfully astonished tone.

„We have every right. An organized meeting for religious purposes is against the law Mr. Jones and you know it. You belong to an illegal religious group and we're taking you into custody. "

As they escort him through the corridor, there, like vipers are the paparazzi. The blinding flash of their cameras turns D into fresh drawn bate for the news sharks. D's arrest is far more newsworthy than the honors that are being bestowed upon the recipients and would more than likely overshadow the event.

      As D is being rushed through the corridor he's bombarded with an array of questions,

„Is it true Mr. Jones that you are a practicing Jehovah's Witness? "

„Is there any statement you'd like to make Mr. Jones? "

„Will you be back in time for the after-party Mr. Jones? "

With that question laughter brakes out amongst them and D never felt so defiled and humiliated in his entire life. He is now finally experiencing the other side of the cutting edge of the presses sword. Most often they had used it to carve a successful career for him. Now he's the object of their virulent malevolence.

„We don't want any religious crony songbird chirping here tonight. Good riddins. ", is the last remark D hears from a man before they push him head last into the dark vehicle that drove him off. "

      When they arrive at the station he's finger-printed, mugged, and booked for obstructing justice. Then the interrogation begins.

      They let him wait it seems, to him for hours sitting on a metal chair, in a dark room, on one side of a table with a desk lamp that's slightly tilted to send some of

its glare into his eyes. All of a sudden one of the men who arrested him enters.
„Where's my lawyer? ", D asks.
„He hasn't gotten here yet. Maybe he got caught up in traffic. "
„It must be the middle of the night. There is no traffic. ", D retorts.
„Well, maybe he went back to bed. "
„You sent him somewhere else, didn't you. ", says D.
Silence.
„Listen D, that is your name right? Or should I call you Daniel? Well you're in
the lion's den now Daniel and you're either going to cooperate with us or its going
to get mighty uncomfortable for you here. "
A cold shiver shot through D's body from head to foot.
„The rest of the world seems to have gotten the picture, but you damn J.W.'s are
a stubborn lot. I'm here to see to it that your organization gets shut down
completely and for good. And you're going to help me, aren't ya Daniel? "
It wasn't so much what he said, but the way he said it that made D livid and gives
him a surge of courage. D looks at him directly with squinted eyes and shot him
a look that says without uttering one word,
„You haven't met or known stubbornness until you've met me. "
It makes the agent take a step backwards.
„Where is Michael Callan? " he shouts.
D remains silent.
„Where are your meetings held? "
The agent kept asking and intermittently shouting question after question. Yet D
remains silent throughout the barrage of questions. The agent then leaves.

    It seems like forever before another man comes in and escorts him to the
men's room where they remove his handcuffs and let him relieve himself. As
soon as he's finished they place him back in the room. D's thoughts drift off to
Michael and Sophia as he hoped and wondered if they've followed his
instructions and are now on their way to safety. He assumes they did or else
they would not have continued with this sort of interrogation. He wishes he had
taken Michaels advice not to attend the ceremonies, to have stopped performing
altogether, but.......... it was too late for that now.
A new agent appears now with a different approach to extracting information.
„How are you D? ", he says in a smooth toned voice.
„I really don't want to see you suffer, so why don't you just tell us what we want to
know? All you need do is let us know where we can find Michael Callan. Then
when you sign this document stating that you denounce your religion, you're free
to go. It's as easy and simple as that! "
More silence from D. D's eyes follow him while the agent paces the room.
„Come on D, you're not going anywhere until you tell us what we want to know.
You know, nobody knows where you really are. And your lawyer's not coming.
"D's eyes widen.
„We informed him that if he defends you that he'll face disbarment. It's illegal to
defend people who congregate for the purpose of practicing religion. You didn't
know that did ya? "
D's heart begins to pound in his chest as beads of sweat appear on his brow.

„I can see you didn't. "

For the first time D becomes very fearful for his life.

„I'm gonna let you think it over for awhile. We'll be back. "

When the agent leaves the room D begins to silently weep. He realizes he's totally alone. Alone! Alone, he thought again. I am NOT alone. Jehovah is with me. Jehovah his God who he is on a first name basis with is with him. And for the first time since his arrest he begins to pray silently. He feels so weak, but he continues to pray and call on the name of Jehovah, and before he knew it, with his intense heartfelt prayer to the Father he's no longer afraid. He had resolved in his mind and heart that if he should perish here, then so be it. God has the power to resurrect him at Judgment Day. They could kill his body but his soul belongs to Jehovah. And they can't touch it. He had made up his mind that he would never denounce his allegiance to Jehovah God, Jesus, or his fellow brothers and sisters. Above all he swore to himself that he'd never hand Michael over to them.

Once again the agent that had made D sweat enters the room.

„Thought about our proposal D? So what's it going to be?

D becomes irked by the agent's smooth toned haughtiness that he couldn't resist letting a bit of the Damon in him come out.

„I don't give one infinitesimal DAMN about you or your proposal! I will never tell you where Michael is. And as far as denouncing Jehovah, you'll never EVER live to see that happen. ", D says, and then looks upward and silently asks God to forgive his intentional indiscreet outburst.

„O.K. Then, have it your way. "

He opens the door and in walks another man with a doctor's bag. He sets it on the table, opens it, and prepares a hypodermic infusion.

D's eyes widen in intense fear for he absolutely hates injections of any kind.

„No. " D says inadvertently.

But he's handcuffed and helpless.

„No. ", with closed eyes he says again before he silently begins to pray.

„This'll help you tell us whatcha know. "

He opens his eyes again as the man with the needle moves toward him. It must be some kind of truth serum D thinks to himself. Then he begins to do what he does best. He began to sing a kingdom song. And he sang loudly,

„Jehovah is our refuge, Our God in whom we trust......................... "

He kept his mind fixed on the prayerful lyric while the man shot the injection into his vein. The room begins to spin but he keeps his mind thoroughly fixed on the words and melody of that song. Regardless of what they ask him all that comes back to them are the words of that Kingdom Song. Over and over he sings without stopping.

„Give him more. " the agent commands.

„I can't do that. ", says the man who gave D the first injection.

„That's powerful stuff. If he's had any alcohol or is on any type of prescription drugs it could cause him to.......... "

„I don't care. I'm gonna break that little .... resolve if it's the last thing I do. "

D receives another injection and begins to sing the Kingdom Song,

"Life, like a mist, appears for just a day............He will call........."
"My God, he has the voice of an angel.", says the agent who once again gave
him an injection.
The agent begins to question D again and again repeating the same question,
this time producing the beeper that they confiscated along with his backpack
and other personal belongings. But D eventually begins to sing slower and slower,
softer and softer. He holds the beeper in front of D's face which has slumped
down to his chest. The agent lifts his head with one hand and holds the beeper in
front of D's face with the other and shouts,
„What is this for? When did you use it D? Come on, D tell me when in the hell
did you use it? Who did you beep for Christ's sake? "
But it was no use. D had stopped singing and had passed out!

* * * *

It's about four-thirty a.m. when Sophia and Michael arrive at D's home in Lake
Tahoe. They're completely exhausted from the long drive and quickly have a bite
to eat before turning in around seven. Michael having received the signal while
at the secret congregation meeting quickly dispersed all in attendance and drove
a few miles before dumping the beeper in a trash receptacle. Sophia wakens
suddenly at eleven-fifteen and begins to make herself familiar with the
surroundings of D's cottage. D had stocked the place. She quickly decides what
she will prepare for breakfast. Michael, she thought would probably sleep
another two hours having done most of the driving. D's used to all the
entrapments of city living even while in the country. On the desk is a wide
screened laptop. It had been a while since she had checked her email so Sophia
switches the computer on and logs on to her mail provider.
    But as she's about to type in her address and code the bold headlines in front
of her caught her eyes. She brings her hand to her mouth and gasps as she
reads in a state of absolute disbelief.
„Oh, no! Oh God please no! ", she exclaims as she read:
    „The singer/actor Devoreaux D. Jones was found dead in his house in
Bradley, California. The cause of death is not certain, but officials are not ruling
out suicide. Early last evening the entertainer was arrested at the Ahmanson
theatre for obstruction of justice and non-compliance with the law. His body was
found by the singer's father and mentor Joseph Jones around nine-thirty pacific
standard time............".
Sophia couldn't bear to read any further for she knew that D hadn't committed
suicide, but was murdered. She gives way to her tears.
    Michael begins to stir in the bedroom upon hearing Sophia's muted sobs and
asks,
„Are you alright in there honey? "
Sophia brushes back the tears and quickly composes herself before entering the
bedroom where Michael's slowly awakening. As she stands at the doorway
Michael's eyes slowly focus on her and at a glance he notices her somber

disposition. She walks to the bay window, opens the blinds, and the late morning winter sun pours into the room.

„What's happened? ", he asks.

She walks slowly towards him and sits on the bed. Michael embraces her from behind as she begins again to weep.

„It's alright dear. Sweetheart, I'm sure the others made it safely away from the meeting last night. "

„One of us didn't. ", she replies.

„What do you mean, what are you saying? ", says Michael.

„Michael, D............, D is dead. "

Michael shifts from the mattress and sits beside her on the edge of the bed, and then asks,

„What did you say? "

Trying desperately to hold back her tears she recaps,

„They found him in his house this morning dead. I....I read it on the internet news. They said that he....he had been arrested last night in L.A. at the theatre and his father found him dead. They even said he may have committed suicide. "Michael put his arms around Sophia and holds her close as she cries uncontrollably.

Michael's silence is rivaled only by the serene stillness of the countryside that embraced the cottage.

Michael stares straight ahead out of the large bedroom bay windows in a state of shock and disbelief. His thoughts race as he recalls his last conversation with D before he breaks his silence and says,

„He lost his life saving ours. "

He holds her close, and makes an effort to comfort Sophia who was shedding the tears that Michael for the moment could not.

* * * *

Within the next seven months the authorities continue to arrest and persecute those who would not stop their active participation in the organized worship of God Almighty. The government was ruthlessly relentless in their pursuit to halt the remaining remnant of worshippers of Jehovah God still present on earth. Some who exercised the pure worship during this tribulation gave their lives so that many of their faithful brothers and sisters could live. Those whose religion was based on false doctrines had from the start of the Great Tribulation given in to the edicts of the legalized ban on religion. Yet, those who refuse to give up their integrity to God continue to endure under the hardships of the Great Tribulation. The world void of religion is in a state of hopelessness; left alone with only the brutal coldness of the One World United Global Government that now promised all those who dwell on the earth, peace and security.

Sophia gave birth to a son, and as she holds their newborn son in her arms with Michael standing close at her bedside she announces to those gathered, „Dear friends, meet Daniel Lucas Callan. "

Those present and the whole association of brothers throughout t h e world knew that they would one day soon be re-united with their brother Daniel Lucas Devoreaux Jones and the many others who were faithful to God 'til death. This will come to pass at the resurrection, which is the promise of God Almighty, and will soon be the fulfilled promise, as the world is running rapidly headlong toward the great day of Jehovah God at the battle of Armageddon.

THE END

Bibliography:

Scriptures taken from the Holy Bible - New International Version copyright 1973, 1978, 1984 by International Bible Society. Used by permission of the International Bible Society. Eng. Bible NIV 189/190 IBS99-57000/143000

Scriptures taken from the Holy Bible - RSV Old Testament, copyrighted 1952, 1973, 1980
RSV New Testament copyrighted 1946, 1971, 1973 by the Division of Christian Education of the National Council of the Churches of Christ in the U.S.A. ENG. BIBLE RS53C ABS-1986-30,000-
460,000-Na15

Scriptures taken from the New World Translation of the Holy Scriptures –
Rendered from the Original Languages by the New World Bible Translation Committee – Revised 1984- copyright 1961, 1981, 1984, Watchtower Bible and Tract Society of Pennsylvania and International Bible Students Association English (bi12-E

Ebook Cover Design: Ken Johnson & Jeff Bradley Stern

19 God is not a man that he should tell lies,
Neither a son of mankind that he should feel regret.
Has he himself said it and will he not do it,
And has he spoken and will he not carry it out?
- Numbers 23:19

23 They now arranged for a day with him, and they came in greater numbers to him in his lodging place. And he explained the matter to them by bearing thorough witness concerning the kingdom of God and by using persuasion with them concerning Jesus from both the law of Moses and the Prophets, from morning till evening. **24** And some began to believe the things said; others would not believe. **25** So, because they were at disagreement with one another, they began to depart, while Paul made this one comment:

"The holy spirit aptly spoke through Isaiah the prophet to YOUR forefathers, **26** saying, 'Go to this people and say: "By hearing, YOU will hear but by no means understand; and, looking, YOU will look but by no means see. **27** For the heart of this people has grown unreceptive, and with their ears they have heard without response, and they have shut their eyes; that they should never see with their eyes and hear with their ears and understand with their heart and turn back, and I should heal them.'" **28** Therefore let it be known to YOU that this, the means by which God saves, has been sent out to the nations; they will certainly listen to it."

-Acts 28:23-28

9 After these things I saw, and, look! a great crowd, which no man was able to number, out of all nations and tribes and peoples and tongues, standing before the throne and before the Lamb, dressed in white robes; and there were palm branches in their hands. **10** And they keep on crying with a loud voice, saying: "Salvation [we owe] to our God, who is seated on the throne, and to the Lamb."**.....14** So right away I said to him: "My lord, you are the one that knows." And he said to me: "These are the ones that come out of the great tribulation, and they have washed their robes and made them white in the blood of the Lamb. **15** That is why they are before the throne of God; and they are rendering him sacred service day and night in his temple; and the One seated on the throne will spread his tent over them. **16** They will hunger no more nor thirst anymore, neither will the sun beat down upon them nor any scorching heat, **17** because the Lamb, who is in the midst of the throne, will shepherd them, and will guide them to fountains of waters of life. And God will wipe out every tear from their eyes.

Revelation 7:9-17